Rebecca

of
Sunnybrook
Farm

Rebecca
of Sunnybrook Farm

Rebecca of the Brick House

*Rewritten and
re-told for today's reader*

Eric Wiggin
Kate Douglas Wiggin

Published by
Bethel Publishing Company
1819 South Main Street
Elkhart, Indiana 46516

Cover Illustration by Ed French

Printed in the United States of America

ISBN 0-934998-52-3

To Mother, who grew up in
backwoods Maine where she
learned to read at her own
mother Lucy's knee before she
could remember. It was Mother
who read me the Bible before I
could read or write, and she encouraged me to write that others
might read.

CONTENTS

1

JACK-O'-LANTERN

M iss Miranda Sawyer's old-fashioned garden was the pleasantest spot in Riverboro on a sunny July morning for Rebecca to enjoy her summer vacation. Soon she would enter Wareham Academy as a freshman, and she was reveling in her last real freedom. The rich color of the brick house gleamed and glowed through the elms and maples shading the lawn and garden. Luxuriant hop vines and Washington ivy clambered up the copper lightning rod ground cables and wooden water spouts, hanging their delicate clusters or ruddy leaves here and there in graceful profusion. Woodbine transformed the old shed and toolhouse to things of beauty, and the flower beds themselves were the prettiest and most fragrant in all the countryside.

A row of dahlias ran directly around the garden spot — dahlias scarlet, gold, and variegated. In the very center was a round plot where the upturned faces of a thousand pansies smiled amid their leaves, and in the four corners were triangular blocks of sweet phlox over which the butterflies fluttered unceasingly. In the spaces between ran a riot of portulaca and nasturtiums, while in the more regular, shell-bordered beds grew spirea and gillyflowers, mignonette, marigolds, and clove pinks.

The hollyhocks were Miss Sawyer's special pride, and they grew in a stately line beneath her four kitchen windows, their tapering tips set thickly with gay satin circlets of pink or lavender or crimson. *They grow something like steeples,* thought Rebecca, who was weeding the flower bed, *and the flat, round flowers are like rosettes. But steeples wouldn't be studded with rosettes, so if you were writing about them in a composition, you'd have to give up one or the other, and I think I'll give up the steeples:*

> Happy little hollyhock
> Lifting your head,
> Sweetly rosetted
> Out from your bed.

Rebecca had a passion for the rhyme and rhythm of poetry. From her earliest childhood, words had always been to her what dolls and toys are to other children, and now at fourteen she amused herself with phrases and sentences and images as easily as her schoolmates played with the pieces of their jigsaw puzzles. If the heroine of a story took a "cursory glance" about her apartment, Rebecca would shortly ask her Aunt Jane to take a "cursory glance" at her oversewing or hemming. If the villain "aided and abetted" someone in committing a crime, she would before long merrily request the pleasure of "aiding and abetting" in dishwashing or bedmaking. Sometimes she used the borrowed phrases unconsciously. Sometimes she brought them into the conversation with an intense sense of pleasure in their harmony or appropriateness, for a beautiful word or sentence had the same effect upon her imagination as a fragrant bouquet, a strain of music, or a brilliant sunset.

"How are you gettin' on, Rebecca?" called a shrill voice from within.

"Pretty good, Aunt Miranda. Only I wish flowers would come up as thick as this pigweed. What *makes* weeds be thick and flowers thin? I just happened to be stopping to think a minute when you looked out."

"You think considerable more than you weed, I guess, by appearances. How many times have you peeked into that hummingbird's nest?"

"I don't know," Rebecca answered evenly, though irritated for the moment that her eldest aunt was apparently blind to the fact that she was no longer a little girl. "I don't know, Aunt Miranda, but when I'm working outdoors on such a Saturday morning as this, the whole creation just screams to me to stop and come meditate."

"Well, you needn't go if it does!" responded her aunt sharply. "It don't scream to me when I'm rollin' out these doughnuts, and it wouldn't to you if your mind was on your duty."

Rebecca's strong fingers flew in and out among the weeds as she thought, *Creation* wouldn't *scream to Aunt Miranda. It would know she wouldn't come!*

> *Scream on, you bright and glad creation,*
> *scream!*
> *'Tis not Miranda that will hear your cry!*

"Oh, such funny, nice things come into my head out here by myself," she said with a chuckle.

> Rebecca was weeding the hollyhock bed
> When wonderful thoughts
>   came into her head.
> Her aunt was occupied with the rolling pin,
> And the thoughts of her mind were
>   common and thin.

"That won't do because it's mean to Aunt Miranda, and anyway it isn't a good rhyme. I *must* crawl under the syringa bushes and into the shade a minute. It's so hot, and everybody has to stop working once in a while just to get their breath, even if they aren't making poetry."

> Rebecca was weeding the hollyhock bed
> When marvelous thoughts
>   came into her head.
> Miranda was wielding the rolling pin,
> And thoughts at such times
>   seemed to her as a sin.
>
> Cheered by Rebecca's petting,
> The flowers are rosetting,
> But Aunt Miranda's fretting
> Does somewhat cloud the day.

Rebecca could not help herself as the rhymes tumbled throughout her brain.

Suddenly the rumble of wagon wheels and the clop of a heavy horse's hooves broke the silence, and then a voice called out, a voice that could not wait until the feet that belonged to it reached the spot: "Miss Saw-*yer!* Father's got to drive over to North Riverboro on an errand, and please, can Rebecca go, too, as it's Saturday morning and vacation besides?"

Rebecca crawled out from under the syringa bush, eyes flashing with delight at the invitation. Repressing her glee at this glad offer of a holiday from drudgery, she asked politely, "May I go with them, Aunt Miranda? Can I, Aunt Jane? I'm more'n half through the flower bed!"

"If you finish your weeding tonight before sundown I s'pose you can go, so long as Mr. Perkins has been good enough to ask you," responded Miss Sawyer reluctantly. Rebecca had peeled her gingham apron off and was on her way to the pump to wash her hands before Aunt Miranda had finished answering. "How long do you calculate to be gone, Emma Jane?" Miranda asked.

"I don't know. Father's just been sent to see about a sick woman over to North Riverboro. She's got to go to the town poor farm."

This fragment of news speedily brought Miss Sawyer, and her sister Jane as well, outside where Bill Perkins and his wagon were in full view. Mr. Perkins, the blacksmith, was also a selectman and an overseer of the poor. So as a town official he possessed wide and varied information of the kind greedily grasped by the gossips around Riverboro.

"Who is it that's sick?" inquired Miranda.

"A woman over to North Riverboro."

"What's the trouble with her?"

"Can't say."

"Stranger?"

"Yes and no. She's the wild daughter of old Nate Perry. You remember she ran away to work in the factory at Milltown and married a do-nothin' fellow by the name o' John Winslow?"

"Yes. Well, where is he? Why don't he take care of her?"

"They ain't worked well in double harness. They've been rovin' 'round the country, livin' a month here and a month there, wherever they could get work and house-room. They quarreled a couple o' months ago, and he left her. She and her little boy kinda camped out in an old loggin' cabin back in the woods. Then she got terribly sick and ain't expected to live."

"Who's been nursing her?" inquired Miss Jane.

"Lizy Ann Dennett, that lives nearest neighbor to the cabin. But I guess she's tired out bein' a good Samaritan. Anyways, she sent word this morning that nobody can seem to find John Winslow. With Nate and Missus Perry both dead, she ain't got no relations to care for her, and the town's got to be responsible. So I'm goin' over to see how things are. Climb in, Rebecca. You an' Emma Jane crowd back on the cushion an' I'll set forrard. That's the trick! Now we're off!"

"Dear, dear!" sighed Jane Sawyer as the sisters walked back into the brick house. "I remember once seeing Sally Perry in church. She usta come to Sunday school every week with the neighbors. She was a handsome girl, and I'm sorry she's come to grief."

"If she'd kep' on goin' to church an' hadn't looked at the wild boys, she might 'a' been earnin' an honest livin' this minute," said Miranda sourly.

≈ ≈ ≈

The Perkins's horse and wagon rumbled along the dusty country road, and after a while Rebecca remarked, "It's a sad errand for such a shiny morning, isn't it, Mr. Perkins?"

"Plenty o' trouble in the world, Becky, shiny mornin's an' all," that good man replied. "If you want a bed to lay on, a roof over your head, an' food to eat, you've got to work for 'em. If I hadn't labored early an' late, learned my trade, an' denied myself when I was young, I might 'a' been a pauper layin' sick in a loggin' cabin, 'stead o' bein' an overseer of the poor an' a selectman driving along to take the pauper to the poor farm."

"Well," she said, sniffing the fragrance of the new-mown hay and growing hopeful as she did so, "maybe the sick woman will be better on such a beautiful day, and maybe her husband will come back to make it up and say he's sorry."

"I hain't noticed that fellows like John Winslow kin be expected to rescue their damsels in distress," responded the pessimistic blacksmith.

A drive of three or four miles brought the party to a patch of woodland where many of the tall pines and hemlocks had been hewn the previous winter. The roof of a ramshackle hut was outlined against a background of young birches, and a rough path, made in hauling logs to the main road, led directly to its door.

As they drew near, the figure of a woman approached—Mrs. Lizy Ann Dennett, in a gingham dress with a calico apron over it. "Good morning, Mr. Perkins," said the woman, who looked tired and irritable. "I'm real glad you come right over, for she took worse after I sent you word, and she's dead."

Dead! The word struck heavily on the girls' ears. Dead! And their young lives had just begun, stretched on and on, all decked, like hope, in living green. With all the daisies and buttercups waving in the fields and the men heaping the mown grass into fragrant haycocks or tossing it into heavily laden wagons. With the brooks tinkling after the summer showers, with the potatoes and corn blossoming in the fields, the birds singing for joy, and every little insect humming and chirping, adding its note to the blithe chorus of warm, throbbing life.

"I was all alone with her. She passed away suddenly jest about break o' day," said Lizy Ann Dennett. "I sent for Aunt Beulah Day, an' she's been here and laid her out for her buryin'," continued the long-suffering Lizy Ann. "She ain't got any folks, an' John Winslow ain't never had any as far back as I can remember. She belongs to the town now, so you'll have to have her buried and take care of Jacky—that's the boy. He's seventeen months old, a bright little feller, the image o' John, but I can't keep him another day, 'cause I'm all wore out. My own baby's sick, my mother's rheumatiz is extry bad, and my husband is comin' home tonight from his week's work. If he finds a child o' John Winslow's under his roof, I can't say what would happen. You'll have to take him back with you to the poor farm."

"I can't take him this afternoon," objected Mr. Perkins. "I've got to fix a broken rim on Robinson's buggy, an' Squire Bean's got to have his loggin' chain welded by suppertime."

"Well then, keep him over Sunday yourself. He's good as a kitten. John Winslow'll hear of Sal's passin' sooner or later, unless he's gone out of the state altogether. And when he knows his boy's at the poor farm, I kind of think he'll come and claim him. Could you drive me over to the village to see about a coffin, and would you girls mind stayin' here for a spell?" she asked, turning to Emma and Rebecca.

Lizy Ann and Mr. Perkins said no more, but drove off together, only warning them not to stray far away from the cabin and promising to be back in an hour.

There was not a house within sight, either looking up the shady forest road or down it, and the two girls stood watching the wagon out of sight. Then they sat down quietly under a tree, feeling all at once a nameless gloom hanging over their happy summer morning spirits.

It was very still in the woods — just the chirp of a grasshopper now and then, or the note of a bird, or the click of a far-distant mowing machine drawn behind a farmer's horses across a grassy intervale near a forest stream as he made hay in one of the thousands of woodland clearings that open in the northern forest. "We're watching for the dead," solemnly whispered Emma Jane with an excitement which struggled with the morbid thoughts of death. "They watched with my grampa, and there was a great funeral and two ministers. He left two thousand dollars in the bank and a store full of goods and a paper coupon you could cut tickets off twice a year, and they were just like money. And Father sold Grampa's store an' bought his blacksmith shop."

Rebecca did not share either Emma Jane's excitement or her childish awe at the death of this stranger. But, with a sympathy growing out of her friendship for Emma she said, "They watched with my little sister, Mira, too. You remember when she died, and I went home to Sunnybrook Farm? It was wintertime, but she was covered with evergreen boughs and white pinks."

"There won't be any funeral or ministers or singing here," Emma concluded. "Isn't it awful?"

"I suppose there won't be; funerals are for folks with families who care about them. Mama said once that Grampa Sawyer went to President Lincoln's funeral, and it was a grand affair! And oh, Emma Jane," Rebecca continued after some moments, catching her friend's dismay, "no flowers, either. We might get those for her if there's nobody else to do it."

"Would you dare put them on her?" asked Emma Jane in a hushed voice.

"I don't know. It makes me shiver," Rebecca frankly admitted. "But we *could* do it if we were the only friends she had. Let's look inside the cabin."

At the door of the cabin Emma Jane's courage suddenly departed. She held back shuddering and refused either to enter or look in. Rebecca shuddered too, but kept on, drawn by a desire to know and feel and understand the mysteries of existence. Emma Jane hurried softly away from the terrors of the cabin, and after two or three minutes of utter silence, Rebecca issued from the open door, her sensitive face pale and woebegone, tears raining down her cheeks. She ran toward the edge of the wood, sinking down by Emma Jane's side, and covering her eyes, sobbed with grief, "Oh, Emma Jane, she hasn't got a flower, and she's tired and sad looking, as if she'd been hurt and hurt and never had any good times. And there's a tiny, dead baby by her."

Emma Jane blanched for an instant. "Mrs. Dennett never said there were *two dead ones! Isn't that dreadful?* But you've been in once, and it's all over. It won't be so bad when you take in the flowers because you'll be used to it. The goldenrod hasn't begun to bud, so there's nothing to pick but daisies and buttercups. Shall I make a rope of them?"

"Yes," said Rebecca, wiping her eyes. "Yes, that's the prettiest, and if we put it all 'round her like a frame, the undertaker certainly couldn't be so cruel as to throw it away, even if she is a pauper."

"I wonder where her big baby boy is?" Emma put in, changing the subject.

"Perhaps over to Mrs. Dennett's house. She didn't seem sorry a bit, did she?" remarked Rebecca.

"No, but I suppose she's tired sitting up and nursing a stranger. Why are *you* crying, Rebecca?"

"Oh, I can't tell, Emma! Only I don't want to die and have no funeral or singing and nobody sorry for me! I just couldn't bear it!" Rebecca smiled, then laughed aloud, embarrassed at the apparent childishness of her thoughts.

"Neither could I," Emma Jane responded sympathetically. "But I do wish you could write some poetry for her like that you read me out of your Thought Book."

"I could, easily enough," exclaimed Rebecca, pleased by the idea that her rhyming ability could be of any use in such an emergency. "I'll go off and write something while you braid the rope. It's lucky you brought your crochet cotton and I my lead pencil."

In fifteen or twenty minutes she returned with some lines written on a scrap of brown wrapping paper. Standing soberly by Emma Jane, she said, "They're not good lines. I was afraid your father'd come back before I finished, and the first verse sounds exactly like the funeral hymns in the church book. I couldn't call her Sally Winslow — it didn't seem nice when I didn't know her. So I thought if I said 'friend' it would show she had somebody to be sorry for her.

> This friend of ours has died and gone
> From us to heaven to dwell,
> And left behind her little son —
> We pray that he is well.
>
> Her husband has run far away
> And knows not she is dead;
> Oh, bring him back ere 'tis too late,
> To mourn beside her bed.
>
> And if perchance it can't be so,
> Be to her children kind;
> The tiny one that goes with her,
> The other left behind.

"I think that's perfectly elergant!" exclaimed Emma Jane. "It sounds like a minister's prayer in poetry. Shall you sign it with your name like we do our school compositions?"

"No," said Rebecca soberly. "I certainly shan't sign it, not knowing where it's going or who'll read it. I shall just hide it in the flowers, and whoever finds it will guess there wasn't any minister or singing or gravestone or anything, so somebody just did the best they could."

The tired mother with the baby on her arm lay on a long, rough plank table in the cabin, her earthly journey over. And when Rebecca stole in and placed the flowery garland all along the edge of the rude bier, death suddenly took on a more gracious and kindly aspect. The girls' sympathy had softened the rigors of the sad moment. Poor, wild Sal Winslow, in her frame of daisies, looked as if she were missed by an unfriendly world, while the tiny baby, whose heart had fallen asleep almost as soon as it had learned to beat, with Emma Jane's bouquet of buttercups in its tiny, wrinkled hand, smiled as if it might have been loved and longed for and mourned.

"We've done all we can now without a minister," whispered Rebecca. "But what's that?"

A strange sound broke the stillness — a gurgle, a yawn, a merry little call. The two girls ran in the direction from which it came, and there on an old coat in a clump of goldenrod bushes lay a child just waking from his nap.

"It's the other baby that Lizy Ann Dennett told about!" cried Emma Jane.

"Isn't he beautiful! Come straight to me!" Rebecca stretched out her arms.

The child struggled to his feet and tottered, waddling toward the warm welcome of the kindly voice and merry eyes. Rebecca's maternal instincts had been well developed in the large family in which she was next to the eldest. She had always said that there were perhaps a trifle too many babies at Sunnybrook Farm, but, nevertheless, she would have stood loyally by the Japanese proverb: "Whether brought forth upon the mountain or in the field, it matters nothing; more than a treasure of one thousand, a baby precious is."

"You darling thing!" she crooned, as she caught and lifted the child. "You look just like a jack-o'-lantern." The

The tired mother with the baby on her arm lay on
a long, rough plank table in the cabin.

boy was clad in a yellow cotton dress, very full and stiff with starch. His hair was of such a bright gold and so sleek and shiny that he looked like a fair, smooth little pumpkin. He had wide blue eyes full of laughter, a neat little vertical nose, a pert little horizontal mouth with his few white little teeth showing very plainly, and on the whole Rebecca's figure of speech was not so wide of the mark.

"Oh, Emma Jane! Isn't he too lovely to go to the poor farm? If only one of us were married, we could keep him and say nothing and nobody would know the difference! Now that the Simpsons have gone away, there isn't a single baby in Riverboro except the Fogg baby — and the way he bawls!"

"My mother won't keep him, so it's no use to ask her. She says 'most every day she's glad we're grown up, and she thanks the Lord there wasn't but two of us — Ted and me."

"And Mrs. Peter Meserve is too nervous," Rebecca went on, taking the village houses in turn, "and Mrs. Robinson is too neat."

"People don't seem to like any but their own babies," observed Emma Jane.

"Well, I can't understand it," Rebecca answered. "A baby's a baby, I should think, whose ever it is! I think if we haven't got any *private* babies in Riverboro, we ought to have one for the town, and all have a share in it," she chuckled. "But I have a thought. Don't you believe Aunt Sarah Cobb would keep him? She carries flowers to her child in the graveyard every little while. It has a marble cross, and it says, 'Sacred to the memory of Sarah Ellen, beloved child of Sarah and Jeremiah Cobb, aged 17 months.' Why, that's another reason; Mrs. Dennett says this one is seventeen months."

"We might see what Father thinks, and that would settle it," said Emma Jane. "Father doesn't think very sudden, but he thinks awfully strong. If we don't bother him and find a place for the baby ourselves, perhaps he'll be willing. He's coming now; I hear the wheels of his wagon."

Lizy Ann Dennett volunteered to stay and wait for the undertaker, and Jack-o'-Lantern, with his slender wardrobe tied in a bandanna handkerchief, was lifted into the wagon by the reluctant Mr. Perkins and jubilantly held by Rebecca in her lap. Mr. Perkins drove off as speedily as possible, being heartily sick of the whole affair and thinking the girls had already seen and heard more than enough of the seamy side of life that morning.

Mr. Perkins soon found himself mercilessly pelted with arguments against the choice of the poor farm as a home residence for baby Jack-o'-Lantern.

"His father is sure to come back sometime, Mr. Perkins," urged Rebecca. "He couldn't leave this beautiful thing forever. And if Emma Jane and I can persuade Mrs. Cobb to keep him a little while, would you care?"

On reflection, Mr. Perkins said he did not care. He merely wanted a quiet life and enough time left over from public service to attend to his blacksmith's shop. So instead of going home over the same road by which they came, he crossed the bridge and dropped Rebecca, Emma, and their newfound charge at the long lane which led to the Cobb house.

2

THE RIVERBORO AUNTS

Mrs. Cobb, "Aunt Sarah" to the whole village of Riverboro, sat by her window looking for Uncle Jerry, who would be soon driving the noon stage to the post office over the hill. She always had an eye out for Rebecca, too, for ever since she had been a passenger on Mr. Cobb's stagecoach, making the eventful trip from Sunnybrook Farm to the brick house in Riverboro in his company, she had been a constant visitor and the joy of the quiet Cobb household.

Emma Jane, too, was a well-known figure in the lane leading to Aunt Sarah and Uncle Jerry's, but a strange baby was a surprise — a surprise somewhat modified by the fact that Rebecca was a dramatic person and more likely than an ordinary Riverboro girl to appear with unusual outsiders and comrades. Rebecca had once escorted a wandering organ-grinder to the Cobbs' door and begged lodging for him on a rainy night. So on the whole, there was nothing amazing about the coming procession.

The little party — Emma Jane and Rebecca hugging Jack-o'-Lantern — padded up to the hospitable door, and Mrs. Cobb came out to meet them. "Aunt Sarah, dear," Rebecca said, plumping Jack-o'-Lantern down on the grass as she pulled his dress over his feet and smoothed his hair becomingly, "will you please not say a word till I get through, as it's very important you should know everything before you answer yes or no. This baby is named Jacky Winslow, and I think he looks like a jack-o'-lantern. His mother has just died over to North Riverboro, all alone except for Mrs. Lizy Ann Dennett, and there was another little baby that died with her. Emma Jane and I put flowers around them and did the best we could.

"The father—that's John Winslow—quarreled with the mother—that was Sally Perry—and ran away and left her. So he doesn't know his wife and the tiny baby are dead. And the town has got to bury them in a pauper's grave because they can't find the father right off, since he may even have left the state. And Jacky has got to go to the poor farm this afternoon. It seems an awful shame to take him up to that lonesome place with those old people that can't amuse him and raise him right, don't you think?

"If Emma Jane and Alice Robinson and I take most all the care of him, we thought perhaps you and Uncle Jerry would keep him for a little while. You've got a cow for milk and a baby crib, you know," she hurried on pleadingly. "There's hardly any pleasure as cheap as more babies where there's been any before, for baby carriages and cradles don't wear out, and there's always clothes left over from the old baby to begin the new one on.

"Of course, we can collect enough things around the village to start Jacky, so he won't be much trouble or expense," Rebecca went on, hardly stopping for breath. "Anyway, he's past the most troublesome age, and you won't have to be up nights with him, and he isn't afraid of anybody or anything, as you can see by his just sitting there laughing and sucking his thumb, though he doesn't know what's going to become of him. And he's just seventeen months old like dear, little Sarah Ellen. So we thought we ought to give you the refusal of him before he goes to the poor farm. What do you think about it?"

Jacky lurched over on the grass and righted himself with a chuckle, kicking his bare feet about in delight at the sunshine and groping for his toes with arms too short to reach them. This movement entirely upset his equilibrium, which was followed by more chuckles.

Coming down the last of the stone steps, Sarah Ellen Cobb's mother regarded the baby with interest and sympathy. "Poor little mite!" she said, "who doesn't know what he's lost and what's going to happen to him. Seems to me we might keep him a spell till we're sure his father's deserted him for good. Want to come to Aunt Sarah, baby?"

Jack-o'-Lantern turned from Rebecca and Emma Jane and regarded the kind face bravely. Then he held out both his hands, and Mrs. Cobb, stooping, gathered him like a harvest. Being lifted into her arms, he at once tore her spectacles from her nose and laughed aloud. Taking them from him gently, she put them on again, then she set him in the cushioned rocking chair under the lilac bushes beside the steps.

Aunt Sarah took one of his soft hands in hers and patted it, then fluttered her fingers like birds before his eyes and snapped them like castanets. She remembered all the arts she had lavished upon "Sarah Ellen, aged 17 months," years and years ago.

> Motherless baby and babyless mother,
> Bring them together to love one another.

Rebecca knew nothing of this couplet, but she saw clearly that her case was won.

"The boy must be hungry. When was he fed last?" asked Mrs. Cobb. "Just a second longer while I get him some milk, fresh this morning. Then you girls can go home to your dinners, and I'll speak to Uncle Jerry this afternoon. Of course, we can keep the baby for a week or two till we see what happens. Land! He ain't goin' to be any more trouble than a wax doll! I guess he ain't been used to much attention, and that kind's always the easiest to take care of."

At six o'clock that evening, Rebecca and Emma Jane flew up the hill and down the lane again, finding the dear old couple waiting for them in their usual place, the back porch where they had sat so many summers in a blessed companionship never marred by an unloving word. "Where's Jacky?" called Rebecca breathlessly.

"Go up to my bedroom, both of you, if you want to see," smiled Mrs. Cobb, "only don't wake him up."

The girls went softly up the stairs into Aunt Sarah's room. There, in the cradle that had been so long empty, slept Jack-o'-Lantern in blissful unconsciousness of the doom he had so lately escaped. His nightgown and pillowcase were clean and fragrant with lavender, but they were both as yellow with age as saffron, for they had belonged long ago to little Sarah Ellen.

"I wish his mother could see him," whispered Emma Jane.

"You can't tell. Perhaps she's watching from heaven," said Rebecca as they turned reluctantly from the fascinating scene and stole back down the stairs to the porch.

It was a beautiful and happy summer that year, Rebecca's summer after grammar school graduation. Every day of it was filled with excitement and responsibilities. On the Monday after Jack-o'-Lantern's arrival in Riverboro, Rebecca, ever an energetic organizer, founded the Riverboro Aunts Association. The aunts were Rebecca, Emma Jane, and Alice Robinson, and each promised to labor and amuse the visiting baby for two afternoons a week, with Aunt Sarah Cobb gladly agreeing to take the sole responsibility for mornings and Sundays.

A shaky baby carriage was found in Mrs. Perkins's wonderful attic. Shoes and stockings were furnished by Mrs. Robinson. Miss Jane Sawyer knitted a blanket and some shirts. Thirza Meserve, though too young for an aunt, coaxed from her mother some dresses and night-gowns, and she was presented by Rebecca with a green paper certificate allowing her to wheel Jacky up and down the road for an hour under the watchful eye of a full aunt.

Thirza's older sister, Huldah, two years older than Rebecca and Emma Jane, when invited to join the circle of the aunts, announced decidedly that she was too mature for such games. After all, a girl who has been a high school student for two years is certainly too old to mess with babies, she stoutly asserted.

Each girl, under the constitution of the association, could call Jacky "hers" for two days in the week. Great, though friendly, was the rivalry between them, as they washed, ironed, and sewed for their adored "nephew." If Mrs. Cobb had not been the most good-natured woman in the world, she might have had difficulty in managing the aunts. But she always had Jacky to herself the earlier part of the day and after dusk at night.

The days of summer flew by. July had given place to August, and though the Riverboro Aunts still gladly tended Jacky Winslow, Rebecca grew uneasily aware that new arrangements would soon need to be made. Several of them, she among them, would shortly enter Wareham Academy.

Life in the brick house had gone on more placidly of late, for Rebecca was honestly trying to be more careful in the performance of her tasks and duties, and she was slowly learning the power of the soft answer in turning away wrath. Maturity, born both of years and experience, had taught her manners which enabled her, though not always to please Aunt Miranda, at least to win her tolerance.

Miranda had not had, perhaps, quite as many opportunities in which to lose her temper, but it is only fair to say that she had not fully availed herself of all that had offered themselves. If Rebecca had been too messy in her housekeeping as a child, she had become too particular about her person of late, spending, it is to be feared, far too much time in her room fixing her hair and face.

There had been one outburst of righteous wrath occasioned by Rebecca's hospitable habits, which were later shown in a still more dramatic and unexpected fashion. On a certain Friday afternoon, Rebecca was observed taking a bowl of bread and milk upstairs. Aunt Miranda, as always, questioned her, and Rebecca cautiously replied that it was for "a friend."

"What friend have you got up there, for pity's sake?" demanded Aunt Miranda.

"The Winslow baby, come to stay over the weekend, that is, if you're willing. Aunt Sarah says *she* is. Shall I bring him down and show him off? He's dressed in an old suit of Ted Perkins's, and he looks sweet."

"You can bring him down, but you can't show him off for me! You can smuggle him out the way you smuggled him in and take him back to the Cobbs. Where on earth did you get your notions, borrowing that baby for the weekend! You tend him two afternoons a week, as it is!"

"You're so used to a house without a baby you don't know how dull it is," sighed Rebecca resignedly as she moved toward the door. "But at Sunnybrook Farm there was always a nice fresh one to play with and cuddle. There were too many, but that's not half as bad as none at all. Well, I'll take him back. He'll be dreadfully disappointed and so will Aunt Sarah. She was planning to go to Milltown."

"She can un-plan then," observed Miss Miranda without sympathy.

"Perhaps I can go over there and take care of the baby?" suggested Rebecca. "I brought him home so 't I could do my Saturday work just the same."

"You've got enough to do right here, without any borrowed babies to make more steps. Now just give the child some supper and carry it over to Cobbs where it belongs."

"You don't want me to go down the front way. Hadn't I better just come through this room and let you look at him? You've never seen him close up! He has yellow hair and big blue eyes! Aunt Sarah says he takes after his father."

Miss Miranda smiled acidly. "If he takes after his father, he'll take off soon enough, then!"

Aunt Jane was in the linen closet upstairs sorting out the clean sheets and pillowcases for Saturday, and Rebecca sought comfort from her. "I brought Jack-o'-Lantern Winslow home, Aunt Jane, thinking it would help us over a dull Sunday, but Aunt Miranda won't let him stay. Emma Jane has the promise of him next Sunday and Alice Robinson the next. Aunt Sarah wanted me to have him first because I've had so much experience in babies. Come in and look at him sitting up in my bed, Aunt Jane! Isn't he lovely? He's the fat, gurgly kind, not thin and fussy like some babies."

"Are you going to carry that heavy child home in your arms?"

"No, I'm going to drag him in the wooden soapbox wagon. Come baby!" She stretched out her strong arms to the cooing baby, sat down in a chair with the child, turned him upside down unceremoniously, took from his diaper a crooked pin left there earlier in the day by another of the aunts. This she scornfully flung away, walked with him to the bureau, selected a large safety pin, and proceeded to attach his red flannel petticoat to a shirt that he wore. Whether flat on his stomach, or head down, heels in the air, Jack-o'-Lantern knew he was in the hands of an expert. He continued gurgling placidly while Aunt Jane regarded the pantomime with a kind of dazed awe.

"Bless my soul, Rebecca," she exclaimed, "it beats all how handy you are with babies!"

"I ought to be. I've brought up three and a half of 'em," Rebecca responded cheerfully, pulling up the infant's stockings.

Miss Jane stretched out a thin left hand with a slender, worn band of gold with its solitaire diamond on her finger, and the baby curled his dimpled fingers round it and held it fast.

"You wear a ring on your engagement finger, don't you, Aunt Jane? Did you ever think about getting married?"

"Yes, dear, long ago."

"What happened, Aunt Jane?"

"He died — just before."

"Oh!" And Rebecca's eyes grew misty.

"He was a soldier and he died of a gunshot wound, in a hospital down South."

"Oh! Aunt Jane," she said softly. "Away from you?"

"No, I was with him."

"Was he young?"

"Yes. Young and brave and handsome, Rebecca. He was Mr. Carter's brother, Tom."

"Oh! I'm so glad you were with him! Wasn't he glad, Aunt Jane?"

Jane looked back across the half-forgotten years, and the vision of Tom's gladness flashed upon her—his haggard smile, the tears in his tired eyes, his outstretched arms, his weak voice saying, "Oh, Jenny! Dear Jenny! I've wanted you so, Jenny!" It was too much! She had never breathed a word of it before to a human creature, for there was no one who would have understood. Now in a shamefaced way, to hide her brimming eyes, she put her head down on the strong, young shoulder beside her saying, "It was hard, Rebecca!"

Jacky Winslow had cuddled down sleepily in Rebecca's lap, leaning his head back and sucking his thumb contentedly. Rebecca put her cheek down until it touched her aunt's hair, silver-gray but still streaked with auburn, and softly patted her, as she said, "I'm sorry, Aunt Jane!"

Rebecca's eyes were soft and tender, and the heart within her stretched a little and grew, grew in sweetness and intuition and depth of feeling. It had looked into another heart, felt it beat, and heard it sigh. And that is how all hearts grow.

❧ ❧ ❧

Jack-o'-Lantern grew healthier and heartier and jollier as the weeks of the summer slipped away. Uncle Jerry joined the little company of worshipers, and one fear alone stirred in all their hearts—not, as a sensible and practical person might imagine, the fear that the irresponsible father might never return to claim his child, but on the contrary, that he *might* do so!

September came at length with its cheery days and frosty nights, its glory of crimson leaves and its promise of a harvest of pumpkins and ripening corn. Rebecca's matriculation at Wareham was only a weekend away.

Rebecca had strolled down by the Saco River and come up across the pastures for a good-night play with Jacky. Her summer's literary labors had been somewhat interrupted by the joys and responsibilities of aunthood, and her Thought Book was now less frequently drawn from its hiding place under the old loose board in the barn chamber. More and more the world of her childhood was slipping from her grasp as the future, with its learning and toil, loomed on her horizon.

Mrs. Cobb stood behind the screen door with one cheek pressed against the wire netting, and Rebecca could see that she was wiping her eyes. All at once Rebecca's heart gave one prophetic throb and then stood still. She was like a harp that vibrated with every wind of emotion, whether another's grief or her own.

She looked down the lane, around the curve of the stone wall red with woodbine—the lane that would meet the stage road to the station. There, just mounting the crown of the hill and about to disappear on the other side, strode a strange young man, big and tall, with a crop of blondish curly hair showing from under his ratty straw hat. A thin, young woman walked by his side, and perched on his shoulder, wearing his most radiant and triumphant smile, as joyous in leaving Riverboro as he had been during every hour of his stay there, rode Jack-o'-Lantern!

Rebecca gave a cry in which maternal longing and helpless, hopeless jealousy strove for supremacy. Then,

with an impetuous movement she started to dash after the
disappearing trio.

Mrs. Cobb opened the door hastily, calling after her,
"Rebecca, Rebecca, come back here! You musn't follow
where you haven't any right to go. If there'd been anything to say or do, I'd 'a' done it."

"He's mine! He's mine!" stormed Rebecca. "At least
he's yours and mine!"

"He's his father's, first of all," faltered Mrs. Cobb.
"Don't let's forget that. And we'd ought to be glad and
grateful that John Winslow's come to his senses an' remembered he's brought a child into the world and ought to
take care of it. Our loss is his gain, and it may make a
man of him. Come in, and we'll put the baby things away
all neat before your Uncle Jerry gets home."

"Oh, Aunt Sarah, how shall I tell Emma Jane?" Rebecca protested. "What if his father doesn't love him?
What if his stepmother doesn't know how to care for a
child? That's the worst of babies that aren't private — you
have to part with them sooner or later!"

"Sometimes you have to part with your own, too," said
Mrs. Cobb quietly. And though there were lines of sadness
in her face, there was neither rebellion nor bitterness as
she folded up the sides of the old cradle, preparing to put
it away once again in the attic. "I shall miss Sarah Ellen
now more'n ever. Still, Rebecca, we mustn't complain.
Remember that 'the LORD gave, and the LORD hath taken
away; Blessed be the name of the LORD.'"

"Sometimes . . . sometimes, Aunt Sarah," said Rebecca
brightening, "you have to part with your childhood, I
guess."

Sarah Cobb only ran her bony fingers through
Rebecca's black hair and thought the girl at her feet was
growing into womanhood.

3

REBECCA'S SKY WIDENS

The time so long and eagerly awaited had come, and Rebecca Randall was a student at Wareham Academy. From September to Christmas, Rebecca was to go to and fro daily on the steam train from the brick house in Riverboro, and then she would board in the Wareham dormitory full-time during the three coldest months.

Persons who had enjoyed the social advantages of foreign courts, or had mingled freely in the intellectual circles of great universities, might not have looked upon Wareham as an extraordinary experience. But it was as much of an advance upon Riverboro as Riverboro had been upon Sunnybrook Farm.

Rebecca intended to complete the four-year course in three, as it was felt that when she had attained the ripe age of seventeen she must be ready to earn her own living and help in the education of the younger children of Maine. While she was wondering how this could be successfully accomplished, some of the other girls who had been her chums at the Riverboro Village School were scheming how they could meander through the four years and come out at the end knowing no more than at the beginning.

To pretty Emma Jane Perkins, the blacksmith's daughter and Rebecca's best friend, one book was as bad as another, and she could have watched the libraries of the world sinking into ocean depths and have eaten her dinner happily at the same time. Emma passed her entrance exams in only two subjects, and she went cheerfully into the preparatory department with her five conditions of probation, intending to let the stream of education play gently over her mental surfaces and not get any wetter than she could help. Though Emma Jane was not an especially brilliant student, her dogged, unswerving loyalty to Rebecca — her gift of devoted, unselfish love for her friend — had motivated her to beg her father to pay for her education at Wareham. Love and devotion, after all, are talents of a sort, and may possibly be of as much value in the world as a sense of mathematics or a faculty for foreign languages.

Wareham was a pretty New England village of white clapboard houses, with a broad main street shaded by great maples and elms. It had a drugstore, a blacksmith shop, a hardware store, a plumbing shop, several general merchandise stores, two churches, and many boarding houses. But the town's principal interests gathered about its academy. This seat of learning, though in most respects typical of academies scattered across Maine, had by careful administration achieved over the decades a reputation which made its graduates welcome in the ivy halls of Bowdoin or Harvard. There were boys and girls gathered there from all parts of the county and state, and they were of every kind and degree as to birth, position in the world, wealth, or poverty.

There was opportunity at the academy for foolish and imprudent behavior, but on the whole, surprisingly little advantage was taken of it. Among the older students, there was a certain amount of going to and from the trains in couples; some carrying of heavy books up the hill by the sterner sex for their schoolmates.

Too, there were occasional bursts of silliness on the part of heedless and precocious girls, among whom was Huldah Meserve, who had managed to attract the attention of several upper-class young men. She was friendly enough with Emma Jane and Rebecca, but she grew less and less friendly as time went on. Huldah was extremely pretty, with a profusion of auburn hair and a few very tiny freckles, to which she constantly alluded as no one could possibly detect them without noting her porcelain skin and curling lashes. She had merry eyes, a somewhat too plump figure for her years, and she was popularly supposed to be a fascinating conversationalist.

Riverboro, being poorly furnished with suitable young men — extremely few from wealthy families — Huldah intended to have as good a time during her years at Wareham as circumstances would permit. Her idea of pleasure was an ever-changing circle of admirers to fetch and carry for her, the more publicly the better. Incessant chatter and laughter and vivacious conversation, made eloquent and effective by arch looks and telling glances, were her game also. She had a habit of confiding her conquests to less fortunate girls and bewailing the incessant havoc and damage she was doing — a damage she avowed herself as innocent of, in intention, as any newborn lamb.

It does not take much of this sort of thing to wreck an ordinary friendship, so before long Rebecca and Emma Jane sat in one end of the railway train in going to and from Riverboro, and Huldah, who though she boarded at Wareham, ordinarily went home on Fridays, occupied the other with her court. Sometimes this was brilliant beyond words, including a certain youthful Don Juan, who on weekends expended thirty cents on a round-trip ticket and traveled from Wareham to Riverboro merely to be near Huldah. Sometimes, too, her circle was reduced to the popcorn-and-peanut boy of the train, who seemed to serve every purpose in default of better game.

Rebecca was normally unconscious of romantic interests. Boys were good comrades but no more. She liked reciting in the same class with them; everything seemed to move better with boys as academic competitors. But from precocious flirtations she was protected by her ideals. There was little in the lads she had met thus far to awaken her fancy, for her mind habitually fed on better bread. Huldah's schoolgirl romances, with their wealth of commonplace detail, were not the stuff her dreams were made of, when dreams did indeed flutter across the sensitive plate of her mind.

Among her teachers at Wareham one influenced Rebecca profoundly—Miss Emily Maxwell, with whom she studied English literature, composition, and Latin. Miss Maxwell, the niece of one of Maine's former governors and the daughter of a prominent Portland physician, was the most remarkable personality in Wareham. That her few years of teaching happened to be in Rebecca's time was the happiest of all chances. There was no indecision or delay in the establishment of their relationship. Rebecca's heart flew like an arrow to its mark, and her mind, meeting its superior, settled at once into an abiding attitude of respectful homage.

It was rumored that Miss Maxwell "wrote." And this word, when uttered in a certain tone, was understood to mean not that a person had command of penmanship but that she had appeared in print in a magazine.

"You'll like her; she writes," whispered Huldah to Rebecca the first morning at chapel, where the faculty sat in

an imposing row on the front seats. "She writes. But I call her stuck up."

Miss Maxwell's height of achievement — a published author — made Rebecca somewhat shy of her, but she looked on her with admiration. Miss Maxwell's glance around her classroom was always meeting a pair of eager dark eyes. When she said anything particularly good, she looked for approval to the corner of the second row, where every shade of feeling she wished to evoke was reflected on a certain sensitive young face framed in black braids.

One day, when the first essay of the class was under discussion, she asked each new pupil to bring her some composition written during the previous year that she might judge the work and know precisely with what material she had to deal. Rebecca lingered after the others and approached the desk shyly.

"I haven't any compositions here, Miss Maxwell, but I can find one when I go home to Riverboro on Friday. They are packed deep in a trunk in the dark attic, so I won't be able to hunt for them until Saturday when the sun shines through the south window, and it's nearly dark when I get home."

"Carefully tied with pink and blue ribbons?" asked Miss Maxwell, with a whimsical smile.

"No," answered Rebecca, shaking her head decidedly. "I wanted to use ribbons, because all the other girls did, and they looked so pretty. But I used to tie my essays with twine strings on purpose. And the one on 'Solitude' I fastened with an old shoelacing just to show what I thought of it."

"'Solitude'!" laughed Miss Maxwell, raising her eyebrows. "Did you choose your own subject?"

"No. Miss Dearborn thought we were not old enough to find good ones."

"What were some of the others?"

"'Fireside Reveries,' 'Grant as a Soldier,' 'Reflection on the Life of Russell Conwell,' 'Buried Cities.' I can't remember any more now. They were all bad, and I can't bear to show them. I can write poetry easier and better, Miss Maxwell."

"Poetry!" she exclaimed. "Did Miss Dearborn require you to do it?"

"Oh, no. I always did it, even at the farm. Shall I bring all I have? It isn't much."

Rebecca took the blank book in which she kept copies of her poetic scribblings and left it at Miss Maxwell's apartment door, hoping that she might be asked in and thus obtain a private interview. But a housemaid answered her ring, and she could only walk away, disappointed.

A few days afterward she saw her black-covered book on Miss Maxwell's desk and knew that the dreaded moment of criticism had come, so she was not surprised to be asked to remain after class. The room was quiet; the red leaves rustled in the breeze and flew in at the open window, bearing the first compliments of the season. Miss Maxwell came and sat by Rebecca's side on the bench. "Did you think these were good?" Miss Maxwell asked, giving her the verses.

"Not so very," confessed Rebecca, "but it's hard to tell all by yourself. The Perkinses and the Cobbs always said they were wonderful, but when Mrs. Cobb told me she thought they were better than Longfellow's I was worried, because I knew that couldn't be true."

This remark confirmed Miss Maxwell's opinion of Rebecca as a girl who could hear the truth and profit by it.

"Well, my child," she said smilingly, "your friends were wrong and you were right. Judged by the proper tests, they are pretty bad."

"Then I must give up all hope of ever being a writer!" sighed Rebecca, who was tasting the poison bitterness of hemlock and wondering if she could keep the tears back until the interview was over.

"Don't go so fast," interrupted Miss Maxwell. "Though they don't amount to anything as poetry, they show a good deal of promise in certain directions. You almost never make a mistake in rhyme or meter, and this shows you have a natural sense of what is right — a 'sense of form,' poets would call it. When you have a little more experience — in fact, when you have something to say, I think you may write very good verses. Poetry needs knowledge and vision, experience and imagination, Rebecca. You may not have the first three yet, but I rather think you have a touch of the last."

"Must I never try any more poetry, not even to amuse myself?"

"Certainly you may. It will only help you to write better prose. Now for the first composition I am going to ask all the new students to write a letter giving some description of the town and a hint of the school life."

"Shall I have to be myself?" asked Rebecca.

"What do you mean?"

"A letter from Rebecca Randall to her sister Hannah at Sunnybrook Farm, Temperance, or to her Aunt Jane at the brick house, Riverboro, is so dull and stupid if it is a real letter. But if I could pretend I was a different girl altogether and write to somebody who would be sure to understand everything I said, I could make it nicer."

"Very well, I think that's a delightful plan," said Miss Maxwell. "And who will you suppose yourself to be?"

"I like heiresses very much," replied Rebecca contemplatively. "Of course, I never saw one, but interesting things are always happening to heiresses, especially to the golden-haired kind. My heiress wouldn't be vain and haughty like the wicked sisters in *Cinderella*. She would be noble and generous. She would give up a grand school in Boston because she wanted to come here where her father lived when he was a boy, long before he made his fortune. The father is dead now, and she has a guardian, the best and kindest man in the world. He is rather old, of course, and sometimes very quiet and grave. But sometimes when he is happy he is full of fun, and then Evelyn is not afraid of him. Yes, the girl shall be called Evelyn Abercrombie, and her guardian's name shall be Mr. Adam Ladd."

"Do you know Mr. Ladd?" asked Miss Maxwell in surprise.

"Yes, he's my very best friend," cried Rebecca delightedly. "Do you know him, too?"

"Oh, yes, he is a trustee of this school, you know, and he often comes here. But if I let you 'suppose' any more, you will tell me your whole letter and then I shall lose a pleasant surprise."

What Rebecca thought of Miss Maxwell we already know. How the teacher regarded the pupil may be gathered from the following letter written two or three months later.

December 1st

My Dear Father,

As you well know, I have not always been enthusiastic about teaching. The task of cramming knowledge into these self-sufficient, inefficient youngsters discourages me at times. If my department were geography or mathematics, I believe I should feel that I was accomplishing something, for in those branches, application and industry work wonders. But in English literature and composition one yearns for brains, for appreciation, for imagination!

Month after month I toil on, opening oyster after oyster, but seldom finding a pearl. Fancy my joy this term when, without any violent effort at shell-splitting, I came upon a rare jewel of satin skin and beautiful luster! Her name is Rebecca, and she looks not unlike Rebekah at the well in our family Bible. Her hair and eyes are so dark as to suggest a strain of Italian or Spanish blood though she says her father, now deceased, was French Canadian. She is nobody in particular. She has no family to speak of, no money, no education worthy the name, has had no advantages of any sort. But Dame Nature has flung her into the breach and said:

> This child I to myself will take;
> She shall be mine and I will make
> A Lady of my own.

Think of reading Wordsworth's "Lucy" to a class, and when you finish seeing a fifteen-year-old pair of lips quivering with delight and a pair of eyes brimming with comprehending tears!

Fancy my joy of finding a real mind—of dropping seed in a soil so warm, so fertile, that one knows there are sure to be foliage, blossoms, and fruit all in good time! I wish I were not so impatient and so greedy of results! I am not fit to be a teacher. No one is who is so scornful of dull wits as I am.

My pearl writes quaint little countrified verses of her childhood at a place called Sunnybrook Farm, or of growing up with her aunts in the brick house in Riverboro. They are doggerel, but somehow or other she always contrives to put in one line, one thought, one image, that shows you that she is, quite unconsciously to herself, in possession of the secret of poetry. Good-by. I'll bring Rebecca home with me some Friday and let you and Mother see her for yourselves.

Your affectionate daughter,

Emily

4

REBECCA'S WORLD

R ebecca's world—her physical surroundings and the people who filled it—consisted of the little village of Riverboro in the valley of the Saco River, where she lived with her aunts in the brick house, and Wareham Academy, a half-hour daily commute by steam train into the foothills of the White Mountains of western Maine. Behind her lay her childhood, "ages and ages ago," to her recollection. In her past was dear Sunnybrook Farm outside Temperance, an even tinier and more insignificant village than Riverboro. Here she had left her mother, the widow Aurelia Randall, brothers John and Mark, little sisters Jenny and Fanny, and big sister Hannah. Here, too, beneath a weeping willow shading the hillside sloping down to the brook which watered the farm, lay the bodies of the father, Lorenzo Randall, and little sister Mira.

Rebecca's spinster aunts, Miranda, the eldest, and Jane, just younger than Aurelia—known around Riverboro as "the Sawyer girls"—had taken on Rebecca's education, which they believed would "be the making of her." The Sawyer sisters had been bequeathed the brick house, a quarter section river valley farm, along with another quarter section of forest—half a square mile in all—a quarter century earlier by their father, Deacon Israel Sawyer. His own grandfather had, a century before that, strode up the Saco Valley with only his gun, his ax, and his knife to stake his claim as his mustering-out pay from the Continental Army — King George's Redcoats having been happily disbanded to England, and General George Washington having been installed by Congress as our first president.

The brick house was without a doubt the grandest estate in the Saco Valley, though since the days of Rebecca grander houses have arisen along the river. Its two-and-a-half stories rose amongst grand old elms near the road from Maplewood where it bends to cross the bridge and enter the village from the east. Back of the brick house was attached a long shed, or ell, spacious enough to admit a carriage in foul weather and with ample storage for firewood for the long Maine winters, garden tools, trunks, harness, and cast-off furniture. Beyond the ell and attached to it, in the fashion of rural upper New England, was the cedar-shingled cattle and horse barn. This was a grand, heavily timbered structure, framed of hand-hewn beams and boarded with wide planks of virgin pine two feet and more wide.

The Sawyer pasture stretched to the Saco, and the fields and woodlands extended beyond. The fields spread behind the row of houses that faced the south side of Riverboro's only street; and by crossing these fields and pastures, Rebecca, when younger, cut her daily trudge to school in half.

On the west edge of Riverboro Village stood the school, a one-room affair with its broad yard, bare save for a lonesome white pine which served as a support for a swing, and a double outhouse behind. Across the road from the school and halfway up a rocky hill, rose Tory

Hill Meeting House, so named because it stood on the site of a log fortress hastily erected by some of King George's supporters during the Revolution. This grand old white-clapboard edifice, with its spire and bell, had been erected by Puritan Congregationalists in Great-great-grandfather Sawyer's day—a fact which Aunt Miranda Sawyer was fond of reminding visitors to the brick house, pointing with pride to the copper weathercock which her own ancestor had placed on its towering steeple. The church was nominally Congregationalist, but ministers of Baptist, Methodist, or Presbyterian persuasion sometimes held the pulpit, so long as they were delicately judicious about the theological sensibilities of their parishioners.

Rebecca's first and most steadfast friend in Riverboro was Mr. Jeremiah Cobb. It was he who had been the coach driver on the day Aurelia Randall had entrusted her ten-year-old child to his care for the stagecoach ride from Maplewood, the last leg of the journey from Sunnybrook Farm in Temperance. Mr. Cobb had gradually become "Uncle Jerry" in those early months when close-minded Aunt Miranda was trying her best to bring up this undisciplined, wide-eyed waif "by hand." It was Uncle Jerry who had comforted Rebecca when, punished for wearing her newest treasure, a new pink dress, to a school program in her aunts' absence, she had run away from the brick house, determined to return to Sunnybrook and send Hannah to be educated by the aunts in her stead.

Uncle Jerry and his wife, Aunt Sarah Cobb, became Rebecca's dear and satisfying friends. A visit from Rebecca always sent them into a twitter of delight. Her merry conversation and insightful comments on life in general fairly dazzled the old couple, who hung on to her lightest word as if she had been a prophet.

Aunt Sarah flew to the pantry and cellar whenever Rebecca's slim, lithe shape first appeared on the crest of the hill, and a jelly tart or a frosted cake, a cookie or a doughnut was sure to be forthcoming. "I've got to watch my figure," Rebecca often complained, after she had become a student at Wareham. But "A girl who's gettin' an education needs to eat" always settled matters with Aunt Sarah.

The sight of old Uncle Jerry's spare figure in its clean white shirtsleeves always made Rebecca's heart warm when she saw him peering longingly from the kitchen window. Before the snow came, many was the time he had come out to sit on his woodpile to see if by any chance she was mounting the hill that led to their house. In the autumn Rebecca was often the old man's companion while he was digging potatoes or shelling beans. And during her winter holidays from Wareham, when a younger man was driving the stagecoach over the icy roads, Rebecca sometimes stayed with Uncle Jerry while he did his evening milking.

Though Rebecca's days were now spent in studying and commuting, commuting and studying—for the academic course at Wareham Academy was rigorous—on Saturday afternoon, when the yelloweye beans had been stirred for the fortieth time, the cat had been fed, and the parlor dusted for Sunday, Rebecca would often take her aunts' leave and slip over to spend an hour or two with this dear couple, parents to none, but grandparents to this "half-orphan" girl.

It is safe to say that Uncle Jerry was the only creature in Riverboro who possessed Rebecca's entire confidence, the only being to whom she poured out her whole heart, with its wealth of hopes and dreams and vague ambitions. Though others, such as Aunt Jane and Minister Baxter's wife, did share Rebecca's spiritual interests, only old Uncle Jerry knew her soul well enough to touch the depths of her feelings and her disappointments.

Yet there was a depth in Rebecca which Jeremiah Cobb could not plumb. Rebecca the child he knew, though she had amazed him on that eventful day she had been his passenger on the last leg of her journey from Sunnybrook. Rebecca the teen girl he thought he understood, for he had courted Sarah when she was a girl and married her when she became a woman. But the Rebecca whose imagination and spirit soared beyond the little valley of the Saco, set alight by her books and conversations with those who had traveled afar, caused him to murmur, "I swan! She's the confoundingest creature under heaven!"

At the brick house Rebecca practiced scales and exercises, but at the Cobbs' cabinet organ, she sang like a bird, improvising simple accompaniments that seemed to her auditors nothing short of marvelous. Here she was happy, here she was loved, here she was drawn out of herself and admired and encouraged. *But,* she thought, *oh, if there were somebody who not only loved but understood, who spoke her language, comprehended her desires, and responded to her mysterious longings!* Perhaps in the big world of Wareham Academy there would be people who thought and dreamed and wondered as she did, she mused.

Miranda Sawyer's confidence in her ability to understand Rebecca and supply the needs of the child, and now the girl, was equaled only by her lack of ability to grasp the inmost workings of Rebecca's heart. As the eldest in a family of three girls, Miranda was possessed of a strong will, courage, and a conviction, begotten in her admittedly limited life experiences, that her ways, her opinions, were right.

Miranda, like her ancestors, was possessed of well above average intelligence. And she was gratified to find that her "wild" niece, for all her apparent shortcomings, excelled in the Riverboro district school. Though Rebecca found geometry difficult and algebra preposterous, she readily grasped history, geography, and languages.

Rebecca memorized Longfellow and Whittier at ten and read and quoted Shakespeare at twelve — a fact which caused Miranda to swell with pride at her niece's "larnin'." But she once remarked that Rebecca was "touched in the head" when Rebecca applied literary allusions to the humdrum affairs of life in Riverboro.

Miranda Sawyer could be a generous woman, but only in a manner which suited her narrow opinions. She freely took in Rebecca when her widowed sister could no longer afford to feed her. She gladly paid Rebecca's tuition, board, and daily train fare to Wareham. But it took the ingenuity of both Rebecca and Aunt Jane to get Miranda to agree to buttons and lace for a dress, when hooks and piping trim would do. Rebecca had to trudge her weary, roundabout way up the back stairs to reach her room, because the direct route — the front hall stairs — was carpeted, and carpet, Miranda often pointed out, would wear out and require costly replacement.

If Miranda had music in her soul, it was deeply buried. She knew the hymns of Watts and Wesley, and she could carry a tune in church. But she refused to part with five dollars to have the piano in the sitting room tuned, though Rebecca came from Sunnybrook with ability to play the piano — a talent which she had acquired from her musical father.

One spring day Rebecca discovered that by leaving the window open and striking the very off-key middle C, Robinson's hound would set up a perfect imitation on his distant hill. Miranda's own musical sensibilities thus at last touched, a piano tuner was forthwith engaged to turn misery into melody.

In reality, Jane did not understand her niece very much better than Miranda. The difference between the sisters was that while Jane was puzzled, she was also attracted, and when she was quite in the dark for an explanation of some quaint or unusual action, she was sympathetic as to its possible motive and believed the best. A greater change had come over Jane than over any other person in the brick house, but it had been wrought so secretly and concealed so well that it scarcely appeared to the ordinary observer. Life had now a motive utterly lacking before. Breakfast was no longer eaten in the kitchen, because it seemed worthwhile, now that there were three persons, to lay the cloth in the dining room. It was also a more bountiful meal than before when there was no child to consider.

Each morning was made cheerful by Rebecca's start for the academy, the packing of her books, the final word about umbrella, raincoat, or rubbers, the parting warning and the unconscious waiting at the window for the last wave of the hand as she hurried down the street toward the tiny depot.

Jane found herself taking pride in Rebecca's improved appearance, her rounded throat and cheeks, and her better color. She would often mention the length of Rebecca's hair and comment on its remarkable evenness and luster when Mrs. Perkins bragged on Emma Jane's complexion. She threw herself wholeheartedly on her niece's side when it was a choice between a crimson or a brown wool dress, and she once went through a memorable struggle with Miranda concerning the purchase of a red bird for Rebecca's black felt hat.

No one guessed the quiet pleasure that lay hidden in Jane's heart when she watched the girl's dark head bent over her lessons at night, or dreamed of her joy in certain quiet evenings when Rebecca would read aloud "Hiawatha" or "Barbara Freitchie," "The Bugle Song" or "The Brook."

And when, now a Wareham Academy student, Rebecca brought her leather briefcase of textbooks home to study, Jane thought of her own academy days when she had dreamed of becoming a schoolteacher—yes, even a wife. Jane's narrow, humdrum existence bloomed under the dews that fell from Rebecca's fresh spirit. Her dullness brightened under the kindling touch of the younger mind, took fire from the spark of heavenly flame that seemed always to radiate from Rebecca's presence.

Emma Jane Perkins, "the rich blacksmith's daughter," lived just across the bridge from the brick house, next to the falls and sawmill. Emma Jane had come to the brick house to pay her respects on the very day that Rebecca had arrived in the coach. It was she who, when Rebecca cried in a forlorn fit of homesickness, hugged her tight and cried with her, feeling Rebecca's pain as her own.

Though Emma Jane was a mediocre student who cared little for the contents of Rebecca's beloved books, she was her most loyal, trusted friend. Emma Jane's apparent wealth—new clothes each fall—and her father's status in the community lifted Rebecca, by association, above the plane of ordinary "half-orphanhood" to a level of acceptability in Riverboro society, such as it was.

Blacksmith Bill Perkins was not only prosperous, but he had been elected Riverboro's first selectman, a position of civic responsibility as closely approaching that of mayor as any to be found in Maine country towns. His responsibility for the affairs of the poor in and about

Riverboro gave Rebecca some rare insights into the desperate conditions of some of her less fortunate neighbors.

The Simpson affair was an episode in Rebecca's life which, though she was a teenager at the time, she did not understand, and so she wisely resolved to store it in her memory until age and experience should render it comprehensible. Bill Perkins felt it his civic duty to forcibly remove the "Simpson brood," a family of paupers headed by the usually absent, thievish Abner Simpson, from their home (now owned by the town for nonpayment of taxes) and ship them back to their native Acreville. Rebecca's loyalties were naturally divided in this, for Clara Belle Simpson, a girl her own age, had with Emma Jane Perkins made the third side of a trio from the time Rebecca came to Riverboro until the Simpson family was forcibly removed. Though Clara Belle was not as dear and close a friend as Emma Jane, Rebecca had been her sympathetic confidante when her father had been arrested for another "borrowing" spree, or her mother was distraught over a sick baby or an empty pantry.

It was Clara Belle, too, who had once fished Rebecca out of the mill pond, saving her life. The three girls had been skipping across the pond on slippery, floating logs, and Rebecca had had a log turn beneath her feet, throwing her into the brackish waters. Clara Belle had dragged her ashore and then taken the gasping, sodden Rebecca home and dried her clothes before the Simpson stove, so that Aunt Miranda never learned of the near-tragic incident.

Huldah Meserve and Dick Carter, with Emma Jane and Ted Perkins, were the friends who continued after Rebecca went to board in the Wareham Academy girl's dormitory. Dick had been Rebecca's intellectual competitor in the district school; she always compared her achievements with his, and he returned the compliment.

Pretty, smartly dressed (indeed, often overdressed) Huldah Meserve, though she courted Rebecca's friendship out of a sense of insecurity and a desire for companionship, was jealous of Dick's intellectual interest in Rebecca. Rebecca, for her part, did not return the envy. Her only interest in Dick was in his wits. Boys, to Rebecca, were sometimes interesting playmates; and often, as she grew older and other girls dropped out of school one by one to learn home economics and marry, boys became increasingly her only real competitors in her quest for academic achievement.

Boys were often the only competition, that is, unless you count Miss Emily Maxwell, English and Latin instructor at Wareham and Rebecca's mentor. Miss Maxwell had a bachelor of arts degree from Bowdoin College, and it was whispered that she had almost completed a master's degree as well. She had been to Europe, owned a cottage on an island off Cape Cod, and she was a published author. In Rebecca, Miss Maxwell found a young student who hung on to her every word, her every phrase. Though in her three years' teaching Miss Maxwell had had students who had memorized every grammar rule, in Rebecca she found a student whose active mind sought the souls of the men and women who penned the words counted as *literature*.

The orphaned Abijah Flagg was Squire Bean's chore boy at his farm on the Maplewood Road. Never permitted to attend school since he was thought uneducable, he nevertheless attempted to court the "rich blacksmith's daughter"—an exercise at which he was repulsed by the blacksmith himself until he should "make something of himself."

So in Abijah Rebecca found a willing pupil. He had acquired basic letters from McGuffey's venerable *Primer* when she began to tutor him. And by the time Rebecca had run half her course at Wareham, Abijah had mastered Latin. Marvel of marvels, at twenty this unschooled youth passed the entrance exams at Bowdoin.

It was the minister's wife, young Mrs. Baxter, whom Rebecca sought for spiritual guidance. Pretty in her Boston-bought dresses, Mrs. Baxter suffered from none of the constraints of style which kept other Riverboro women squeezed into the mold of local public opinion. Though modest and chaste as they, she nevertheless occasionally shocked the more staid ladies of the village by wearing dresses more up-to-date than the time-worn patterns produced by the clattering sewing machines of the housewives along the Saco Valley.

Mrs. Baxter knew human nature and the Scriptures, as well. Though she was careful of the Pauline admonition to "keep silence in the churches," she nevertheless often asked her reverend husband at home and passed his advice on to Rebecca — tempered always with some of her own. Since Rebecca often went to the Baxter parsonage for summer tutoring in Latin and French, opportunities for quiet talks with this wise lady were many.

Adam Ladd — "Mr. Aladdin," to Rebecca — appeared on an excursion to North Riverboro when Rebecca and Emma Jane had driven there in Bill Perkins's wagon to sell soap to buy the Simpson's a lamp. Mr. Ladd was rich — rich both in cash and intellect. Although young, he had already become a director of a railway company that built tracks for the iron horse to travel to small towns in Maine. And as a graduate and benefactor of Wareham, Ladd had likewise been elected to its board.

Mr. Ladd, a bachelor, had taken a liking to Rebecca, an affinity which developed after he discovered that they came from similar circumstances. He, like her, had been raised by a frugal aunt. Like Rebecca, he had lost a parent when a small child. And Adam Ladd shared with Rebecca an interest in the world beyond Riverboro, an interest in spiritual matters, and a concern for the welfare of others.

5

CLOVER BLOSSOMS
AND SUNFLOWERS

H ow d' ye do girls?" said Huldah Meserve, peeking in
at the door. "Can you stop studying a minute and
show me your room? Say, I've just been down to the store
and bought me these gloves, for I was bound I wouldn't
wear mittens this winter. They're simply too countrified.
It's your first year here, and you're younger than I am, so
I s'pose you don't mind, but I simply suffer if I don't keep
up some kind of style.

"Say, your room is simply too cute for words! I don't
believe any of the others can begin to compare with it! I
don't know what gives it that simply gorgeous look,
whether it's the full curtains, or that elegant screen, or
Rebecca's lamp. But you certainly do have a faculty for
fixing up. I like a pretty room, too, but I never have a
minute to attend to mine. I'm always so busy on my
clothes that half the time I don't get my bed made up till
noon. After all, having no callers but the other girls, it
don't make much difference. When I graduate, I'm going
to fix up our parlor at home so it'll be simply regal. I've
learned decalcomania, and after I take up luster painting I

shall have it simply stiff with drapes and tidies and plaques and sofa pillows and make Mother let me have my own Franklin stove and receive my friends there evenings.

"May I dry my shoes by your radiator? I can't bear to wear rubbers unless the mud or the slush is simply knee deep. They make your feet look so awfully big. I had such a fuss getting this pair of French-heeled boots that I don't intend to spoil the looks of them with rubbers any oftener than I can help. I believe boys notice a girl's feet quicker than anything. Pug Wilson stepped on one of mine yesterday when I accidentally had it out in the aisle, and when he apologized after class he said he wasn't so much to blame, for my foot was so little he really couldn't see it! Isn't he perfectly darling? Of course, that's only his way of talking, for after all I only wear a number three and a half, but these French heels and pointed toes do certainly make your foot look smaller, and it's always said a high instep helps, too. I used to think mine was almost a deformity, but they say it's a great beauty. Just put your feet beside mine, girls, and look at the difference — not that I care much, but just for fun."

"My feet are very comfortable where they are," responded Rebecca dryly. "I can't stop to measure insteps on algebra days. I've noticed your habit of keeping a foot in the aisle ever since you had those new shoes, so I don't wonder it was stepped on."

"Perhaps I am a little mite conscious of them, because they're not so very comfortable at first, till you get them broken in. Say, haven't you got a lot of new things?"

"Our Christmas presents, you mean," said Emma Jane. "The pillowcases are from Mrs. Cobb, the rug from cousin Mary in North Riverboro, the wastebasket from Ted. We gave each other the bureau and cushion covers, and the screen is mine from Mr. Ladd."

"Well, you were lucky when you met him! Gracious! I wish I could meet somebody like that. The way he keeps it up, too! That screen just hides your bed, doesn't it, and I always say that a bed takes the style off any room — specially when it's not made up — though you have an alcove, and it's the only one in the whole building. I don't see how you managed to get this good room when you're such new boarders," Huldah griped. "I moved in here the first day of school, and they put me in a dump!"

"We wouldn't have, except that Ruth Berry had to go away suddenly on account of her father's death. This room was empty, and Miss Maxwell asked if we might have it," returned Emma Jane.

"The great and only Max is more stiff and standoffish than ever," Huldah snorted. "I've simply given up trying to please her, for there's no justice in her. She is good to her favorites, but she doesn't pay the least attention to anybody else, except to make sarcastic speeches about things that are none of her business. I wanted to tell her yesterday it was her place to teach me Latin, not manners."

"I wish you wouldn't talk against Miss Maxwell to me," said Rebecca hotly. "You know how I feel."

"I know. But I can't understand how you can abide her."

"I not only abide, I *love* her!" exclaimed Rebecca. "I wouldn't let the sun shine too hot on her or the wind blow too cold. I'd like to put a marble platform in her classroom and have her sit in a velvet chair behind a golden table," Rebecca exaggerated, trying to soften her earlier candor.

"Well, don't have a fit! She can sit where she likes for all of me. I've got something better to think of." And Huldah tossed her head.

"Isn't this your study hour?" asked Emma Jane.

"Yes, but I lost my Latin grammar yesterday. I left it in the hall for half an hour while I was having a regular scene with Herbert Dunn. I haven't spoken to him for a week, and I gave him back his class pin. He was simply furious. Then when I came back to the hall, the book was gone. I had to go downtown to buy my gloves and to the principal's office to see if the grammar had been handed in, and that's the reason I'm not busy."

Huldah was wearing a woolen dress that had once been gray, but had been dyed a brilliant blue. She had added three rows of white braid and large white pearl buttons to her gray jacket in order to make it a little more dressy. Her gray felt hat had a white feather on it, and a white tissue veil with large black dots made her delicate skin look brilliant. Rebecca thought how lovely the knot of auburn hair looked under the hat behind, and how the color of the front had been dulled by incessant frizzing with curling irons.

Huldah's open jacket disclosed a galaxy of souvenirs pinned to the dress, a background of bright blue—a small American flag, a button of the Wareham Rowing Club, and one or two society pins. She had been pinning and unpinning, arranging and rearranging her veil ever since she entered the room in the hope that the girls would ask her whose ring she was wearing this week. But although both had noticed the new ornament instantly, wild horses could not have drawn the question from them. With her pretty plumage and her silly cackle, Huldah closely resembled the parrot in Wordsworth's poem:

> Arch, volatile, a sportive bird,
> By social glee inspired;
> Ambitious to be seen or heard,
> And pleased to be admired!

"Mr. Morrison thinks my grammar will be returned, and he lent me another," Huldah continued. "He was rather snippy about my leaving a book in the hall. There was a perfectly elegant gentleman in the office, a stranger to me. I wish he was a new teacher, but there's no such luck. He was too young to be the father of any of the girls, but he was handsome as a picture and had on an awful stylish suit of clothes. He looked at me about every minute I was in the room. It made me so embarrassed I couldn't hardly answer Mr. Morrison's questions straight."

"You'll have to wear a mask pretty soon, if you're going to have any comfort, Huldah," said Rebecca. "Did he offer to lend you his class pin, or has it been so long since he graduated that he's left off wearing it? And tell us now whether the principal asked for a lock of your hair to tuck in his wallet?"

This was all said merrily and laughingly, but there were times when Huldah could scarcely make up her mind whether Rebecca was trying to be witty or whether she was jealous. But she generally decided it was merely the latter feeling—rather natural for an immature girl who had little attention.

"He wore no jewelry but a cameo scarf pin and a perfectly gorgeous ring—a queer kind of one that wound round and round his finger. Oh dear, I must run! Where has the hour gone? There's the study bell!"

Rebecca had pricked up her ears at Huldah's speech. She remembered a certain strange ring, and it belonged to the only person in the world who appealed to her imagination—except Miss Maxwell—Mr. Aladdin. Her feeling for him was a mixture of romantic and reverent admiration for the man himself and the liveliest gratitude for his beautiful gifts. Since she and Emma had first met him when they were peddling soap to buy the Simpsons a banquet lamp, not a Christmas had gone by without some remembrance for them both — remembrances chosen with the rarest taste and forethought.

Emma Jane had seen him only twice, but he had called several times at the brick house, and Rebecca had learned to know him better. It was she, too, who always wrote the notes of acknowledgment and thanks, taking infinite pains to make Emma Jane's quite different from her own. Sometimes he had written from Boston and asked her the news of Riverboro, and she had sent him pages of quaint and childlike gossip, interspersed on occasion with poetry, which he read and reread with infinite relish. If Huldah's stranger should be Mr. Aladdin, would he come to see her, and could she and Emma Jane show him their beautiful room with so many of his gifts in evidence?

When the girls had established themselves in Wareham as boarding pupils, it seemed to them existence was as full of joy as it could hold. This first winter was, in fact, the most tranquilly happy of Rebecca's school life — a winter long to be remembered. She and Emma Jane were roommates, and they had put their modest possessions together to make their surroundings pretty and homelike.

The room had, to begin with, a cheerful red wool carpet and a set of maple furniture. As to the rest, Rebecca had furnished the ideas and Emma Jane the materials and labor, a method of dividing responsibilities that seemed to suit the circumstances admirably. Mrs. Perkins's father had been a storekeeper, and on his death he had left his goods to his married daughter. The molasses, vinegar, and kerosene had lasted the family for five years, and the Perkins's attic was still a treasure house of ginghams, cottons, and Yankee notions.

So at Rebecca's instigation, Mrs. Perkins had made full curtains of unbleached muslin which she had trimmed and looped back with bands of Turkish red cotton. There were two table covers to match, and each of the girls had her study corner. Rebecca, after much coaxing, had been allowed by her protective aunts to bring over her precious lamp, which would have given a luxurious air to any apartment. And when Mr. Aladdin's last Christmas presents were added — the Japanese screen for Emma Jane and the little shelf of books of the English poets for Rebecca — the girls declared that it was all quite as much fun as being married and going to housekeeping.

The day of Huldah's call was Friday, and on Fridays from half past two to four Rebecca was free to take a pleasure to which she looked forward the entire week. She often ran down the snowy path through the pine woods across the road from the academy. And coming out on a quiet village street, she went directly to the large white house where Miss Maxwell rented an apartment. The maid answered her knock, took Rebecca's hat and cape and hung them in the hall, put her rubber overshoes and umbrella carefully in the corner, and then opened the door of paradise. Miss Maxwell's sitting room was lined on two sides with bookshelves, and Rebecca was allowed to sit before the fire and browse among the books to her heart's delight for an hour or more. Then Miss Maxwell would come home from her last class and there would be a precious half hour of chat before Rebecca had to meet Emma Jane at the station and take the train to Riverboro — where her Saturdays and Sundays were spent and where she was washed, ironed, mended, and examined, approved and reproved, warned and advised by stiff old Aunt Miranda in quite sufficient quantity to last her the succeeding week.

On this Friday she buried her face in the blooming geraniums on Miss Maxwell's plant stand, then selected *Romola* from one of the bookcases, and sank into a seat by the window with a sigh of infinite content. She glanced at the clock now and then, remembering the day on which she had been so immersed in *Great Expectations* that the Riverboro train had no place in her mind. The distracted Emma Jane had refused to leave without her, and she had run from the station to look for her at Miss Maxwell's. There was but one later train, and that stopped three miles from Riverboro, so that the two girls appeared at their respective homes long after dark, having had a long, weary walk in the snow.

When she had read for half an hour, she glanced out of the window and saw two figures coming from the path through the woods. The knot of bright hair and the coquettish hat could belong to but one person; and her companion, as the couple approached, proved to be none other than Mr. Aladdin. Huldah was lifting her skirts daintily and picking safe stepping places for the high-heeled shoes, her cheeks glowing, her eyes sparkling under the black and white veil.

Rebecca slipped from her post by the window to the rug before the bright fire and leaned her head on the seat of the great easy chair. She was frightened at the storm in her heart, at the suddenness with which it had come on, as well as at the strangeness of an entirely new sensation. She felt all at once as if she could not bear to give up her share of Mr. Aladdin's friendship to Huldah — Huldah so bright, saucy, and pretty — and such good company when she chose to be! She had always joyfully admitted Emma Jane into the precious partnership, but perhaps unconsciously to herself Rebecca had realized that Emma Jane had never held anything but a secondary place in Mr. Aladdin's regard. Yet who was she herself, after all, that she could hope to be first?

Suddenly the door opened softly and somebody looked in, somebody who said, "Miss Maxwell told me I should find Miss Rebecca Randall here."

Rebecca started at the sound and sprang to her feet, saying joyfully, "Mr. Aladdin! Oh, I had heard you were in Wareham, and I was afraid you wouldn't have time to come and see us."

"Who is 'us'? Your aunts are not here, are they? Oh, you mean the rich blacksmith's daughter, whose name I can never remember," he said merrily. "Is she here?"

"Yes, and she's my roommate," answered Rebecca, who thought her own knell of doom had sounded if he had forgotten Emma Jane's name.

The light in the room grew softer, the fire crackled cheerily, and they talked of many things, until the old sweet sense of friendliness and familiarity crept back into Rebecca's heart. Adam had not seen her for several months, and there was much to be learned about school matters as viewed from her own standpoint. He had already inquired concerning her progress from Mr. Morrison, the principal.

"Well, little Miss Rebecca," he said, rousing himself at length, "I must be thinking of my drive to Portland. There is a meeting of railway directors there tomorrow, and when I come to Maine for a railway directors' meeting, I always take the opportunity to visit the school and to give my valuable advice concerning its affairs, educational and financial."

"It seems funny for you to be a school trustee," said Rebecca contemplatively. "I can't seem to make it fit."

"You are a remarkably wise young person, and I quite agree with you," he answered. "The fact is," he added soberly, "I accepted the trusteeship in memory of my poor little mother, whose last *happy* years were spent here."

"That was a long time ago!"

"Let me see, I am twenty-five — though I fear I have an occasional gray hair. My mother was married a month after she graduated, and she lived only until I was ten. Yes, it is a long way back to my mother's time here, though the school was twenty or thirty years old then, I believe. Would you like to see my mother, Miss Rebecca?" Adam drew a wallet-sized leather book from his inside jacket pocket, nearest his heart.

The girl took the small, brass-hinged leather case gently and opened it to find an innocent, pink-and-white daisy of a face, so confiding, so sensitive, that it went straight to her heart. It made Rebecca feel old, experienced, and maternal. She longed instantly to comfort and strengthen such a tender young thing. "Oh, what a sweet, sweet, flowery face!" she whispered softly.

"That flower had to bear all sorts of storms," said Adam gravely. "The bitter weather of the world bent its slender stalk, bowed its head, and dragged it to the earth. I was only a child and could do nothing to protect and nourish that flower, and there was no one else to stand between her and trouble. Now I have success and money and power while still so young, all that would have kept her alive and happy, and it is too late. She died for lack of love and care, nursing and cherishing, and I can never forget that. All that has come to me seems now and then so useless, since I cannot share it with her!"

This was a new Mr. Aladdin, and Rebecca's heart gave a throb of sympathy and comprehension. This explained the tired look in his eyes, the look that peeped out now and then, under all his light speech and laughter.

"I'm so glad I know," she said, "and so glad I could see her just as she was when she tied that white muslin hat under her chin and saw her yellow curls and her sky-blue eyes in the looking glass. Mustn't she have been happy! I wish she could have been kept so and lived to see you grow up strong and good. My mother is always sad and busy, but once when she looked at brother John I heard her say, 'He makes up for everything.' That's what your mother would have thought about you if she had lived — and perhaps she does as it is."

"You are a comforting little person, Rebecca," said Adam, rising from his chair.

As Rebecca rose, the tears still trembling on her lashes, he looked at her suddenly as with new vision.

"Good-by!" he said, taking her slim brown hands in his, adding, as if he saw her for the first time, "Why, little Rose Red-Snow White Soap is making way for a new girl! Burning the midnight oil and doing four years' work in three is supposed to dull the eye and blanch the cheek, yet Rebecca's eyes are bright and she has a rosy color! Her long braids are looped one on the other so that they make a black letter U behind, and they are tied with grand bows at the top! She is so tall that she reaches almost to my shoulder. This will never do in the world! How will Mr. Aladdin get on without his comforting little friend! He doesn't like grown-up young ladies in flowing gowns and wonderful, fine clothes. They frighten and bore him!"

"Oh, Mr. Aladdin!" cried Rebecca eagerly, taking his jest quite seriously "I am not sixteen yet, and it will be years before I'm a lady. Please don't give me up until you have to!"

"I won't! I promise you that," said Adam. "Rebecca," he continued, after a moment's pause, "who is that young girl with a lot of auburn-red hair who tries to put on citified manners? She escorted me down the hill. Do you know whom I mean?"

"It must be Huldah Meserve. She is from Riverboro."

Adam put a finger under Rebecca's chin and looked into her wide open dark eyes—eyes as soft, as clear, as unconscious of guile, and as childlike as they had been when she was ten. He remembered the other pair of challenging blue ones that had darted coquettish glances through half-dropped lids, shot arrow beams from under archly lifted brows, and he said gravely, "Don't pattern yourself after her, Rebecca. Clover blossoms that grow in the fields beside Sunnybrook mustn't be tied in the same bouquet with gaudy sunflowers. They are too sweet and fragrant and wholesome."

6

WAR GAMES AT WAREHAM

W hat're you doin' after Latin, Becky?" Emma Jane queried, as she and Rebecca waited one Friday afternoon in January in the corridor of Longfellow Hall toward the end of their first semester at Wareham. The previous class was leaving, and the girls were waiting to enter for the final session of the day — and of the semester.

"I've got to walk downtown to the mercantile to purchase a couple of new pens and a notebook. My brother Mark sent me a dollar he earned making Christmas wreaths at Sunnybrook for sale in Temperance. Want to come along?"

"You know I do! I've flunked Latin already, so why stay in our room and study? I'll be lucky if I can remember Cicero from Caesar — or was it Horace?"

Rebecca chuckled aloud, recalling that Emma Jane's first quarter Latin grade hadn't been high enough to qualify her to continue Latin for credit. After some soul searching involving Emma, her parents, Miss Maxwell, and the principal, Mr. Morrison, it had been decided she could profitably remain in Latin as a noncredit course, providing she maintained passing averages in her other subjects. "Silly Em," she said. "You come with me and we'll be back in an hour, in plenty of time for the study bell. The walk will stimulate our brains, and then we can study together — geometry or history, since you've given up on Latin."

"Did I hear you say you're going to the store?" inquired a male voice behind Rebecca and Emma Jane an hour later as they descended the granite steps of Longfellow. It was Pug Wilson, a third-year student who sat in the back row of the Latin classroom with Huldah Meserve and two others who were repeating the course they had failed as freshmen. Rebecca's acquaintance with Pug was extremely casual. Since he was the leader of a crowd of well-heeled scions of wealthy families from Portland's Munjoy Hill district, who considered Wareham Academy only a necessary nuisance between grammar school and Harvard College, country girls from villages like Riverboro and Temperance ordinarily had little to do with them — and the exclusion tended to be mutual, with one or two exceptions.

"We-e-e-e-e-ll, yes," Rebecca answered hesitantly.

"Say, I really *must* hit the books this evening, what with exams coming on next week. So I don't have time to run to the store myself." Pug produced a two-dollar bill. "Drop into the hardware store and pick up a half-pound can of gunpowder for me, will you? Buy yourselves some ice cream with the change," he added with a gallant grin. "I'm going turkey hunting at first light tomorrow morning, and I don't have any bang-bang for my muzzle loader."

"Aren't firearms against the dorm rules?" Emma cut in sharply. Since her father, blacksmith Bill Perkins, was first selectman of Riverboro, Emma Jane Perkins had a keen sense of law and order.

"Of course!" Pug appeared genuinely shocked at the question. "My shooting iron's locked in the dean's closet. I take it out only with permission, and then I must take it straight out of the village and into the fields or woods. Several of the fellows do that. Of course," he added quickly, "we *are* permitted to keep our shot and powder in our bureau drawers. Some of the guys use preloaded shells, but I prefer the old way — it's more sporting."

Rebecca, having grown up with two hunting brothers, had no qualms about hunting. Though John and Mark had been boys when she had left Sunnybrook, already the Randall boys were known in the neighborhood for their Nimrod-like marksmanship with their slings. Since then, Rebecca and Emma, in fact, had on several occasions tramped with Emma's neighbor, Abijah Flagg, through the poplar thickets behind Squire Bean's back pasture as Abijah hunted quail. They had even plucked and dressed them for him, he being disdainful of the dirty work following the manly sport of hunting. So, "Sure, I'll have it back by four o'clock," Rebecca answered pleasantly.

"Good girl, Becky," Pug replied superciliously. "Just pop the can of bang-bang into my pigeonhole when you pick up your afternoon mail. I'll get it after supper." Pug rightly assumed that Rebecca would spend the weekend on campus. For with the dead chill of winter setting in, her weekends at the brick house had become less frequent, and her need to study for semester finals virtually dictated that she spend Saturday in the library or in her room. Pug, however, suffered from no such preexam compunction.

"Goin' gunnin', are ye, Miss?" inquired the hardware storekeeper jocularly as he carefully weighed the black gunpowder on his balance scales.

"No — not exactly," Rebecca answered. "Actually, I'm buying it for . . ."

"Yer brother? You don't have t' be modest, nowadays. I've got two daughters as shoots anything with fur or feathers. Good shots, too. Las' fall my youngest—she's only fourteen—brought down a buck at three hundred yards with my new .45–70."

"My brother *does* hunt," Rebecca told him truthfully. "And I fired a shotgun once. But this is for a friend."

"I see. That kind. Friendships can get explosive." The hardware man winked at Emma Jane as he screwed the tin lid on a small, stiff pasteboard can, on which he'd written in crayon, "Black Powder—8 oz." He then passed it to Rebecca. "See that it doesn't get wet, an' don't set it near no hot stoves or on radiators. Too dry powder kin really pack a mean wallop."

Rebecca felt her small ears burning beneath her black braids and tam as she paid for the gunpowder. His joke had been at her expense, and though ordinarily not easily embarrassed, Rebecca felt certain that the color in her cheeks must betray her uncomfortable sense of wrongdoing. Uneasily she remembered that Pug had been too busy to walk to the hardware store, but not too busy to plan a turkey hunting trip for Saturday when others would be studying for their finals. *Next time Pug Wilson can buy his own black powder,* Rebecca told herself.

The pharmacy, next up the street toward the academy campus, had added a soda fountain, a novel feature for New England hill towns, during the fall of Rebecca's first year at Wareham. Ice cream was made there daily from the milk of local dairy herds in months when sufficient ice could be obtained. And since Maine's commodious ice-houses supplied northeastern cities from Boston to New York with Kennebec ice year-round, the supply was ordinarily plentiful. Here Rebecca purchased a strawberry cone for herself and a chocolate one for Emma Jane. Her packets safely inside the deep pockets of her long wool winter coat, Rebecca, with Emma Jane, hurried along the frozen walkways toward the campus on the hill.

The Wareham Academy campus lay between two highways coming into the village from the foothills of the White Mountains. The roads joined at a fork just above the business district, and the triangular space between them consisted of a small park with a granite monument honoring the Civil War dead. This stone obelisk had been silently guarded for a quarter of a century in Rebecca's time by a magnificent Confederate cannon, abandoned by Lee's retreating troops in McClellan's rout at Antietam, and brought by rail to Maine after the War Between the States. It, and many others like it, now graced the commons of New England towns as the grim trophies of victory.

This mighty, silent gun was continually kept free of rust, polished to a sheen by the corduroy breeches of village urchins who slid up and down its grand barrel. The more imaginative youth of the town pretended they were blasting Rebel snipers out of the belfry of First Church at the far end of the village, fully half a mile distant. The old gun in those days still had its elevator gears and ratchet; indeed, since a cannon is little more than a giant musket, any child with a basic knowledge of gunnery could easily have reduced First Church's sanctuary to splinters, a fact not lost on some of Wareham's more nervous mothers, especially when they considered that the mound of iron balls before the great siege gun were the exact diameter of the weapon's yawning muzzle.

"Rebecca!" Emma Jane exclaimed as the girls approached the green with its midwinter blanket of white. "Look!" Penelope Bennett was standing in ankle-deep snow with her new Kodak, a Christmas present from her parents, taking snapshots of a series of students who posed in turn before the cannon. Penelope was one of the wealthy Munjoy Hill crowd, and now that cameras had broken out of the photographer's portrait studio and entered popular use, she was the first at the academy to own one. "Let's pose for Penny's Kodak!" shrieked Emma Jane.

"Whatever you say, Em. We've got a few minutes before the study bell." Rebecca and Emma stood arm in arm before the grand old war gun as Penelope framed them in her viewfinder and snapped the shutter. Rebecca then impetuously dusted the snow from the gun barrel with a mittened hand and mounted the mighty smoothbore with the agility of a squirrel climbing an oak.

It may have been her natural bent for stage acting, or perhaps a happy thought of candid portraiture for posterity that motivated her—whatever. Rebecca fished the can of gunpowder from her pocket, stretched flat on her stomach on the cannon's barrel, and kicked her heels up. She held the can of powder with its label displayed and poised it as if to roll it down the gun's throat, then raised her head, grinning merrily at the camera lens as Penelope took her picture. "Your Aunt Miranda will have a fit when she sees that photo," warned Emma Jane.

Rebecca sat up, struck a jaunty sidesaddle pose, and put the can away before a second shot from Penelope's Kodak. "This one's for my aunts," she said decidedly.

"When will the photos be ready?" Emma asked as soon as the picture-taking session was finished.

"First thing Monday morning, soon's I can get a break from exams. The druggist now has his own darkroom, so he doesn't have to send the film to Portland to be developed. I shall have the best ones enlarged for framing, if some of you girls want to pay the expense."

"Yes, do!" came a chorus from the crowd, almost in unison.

Later in their room, Rebecca deposited the can of gunpowder on the double dresser she shared with Emma Jane, intending to place it in Pug Wilson's mailbox outside the dining room when they went to supper. No sooner had Rebecca and Emma Jane settled into drilling each other on the Pythagorean theorem and equilateral triangles than Huldah Meserve walked in, the door being open to let the heat from their radiator circulate, since the dormitory was quiet for the two-hour afternoon study session.

"What's the matter Huldah?" Rebecca asked evenly, masking her displeasure at being interrupted.

"I've misplaced my Latin book."

"Again? Wasn't it last week—or was it last month you let one of those Munjoy Hill boys borrow it?" Rebecca's tone now reflected both amusement and irritation.

"I've never found mine. But if I do, I shall drop it down the well," sardonically commented Emma Jane.

"You've lost yours, too?"

"Not really," laughed Emma. "But if you wish to borrow a Latin book you surely may have mine 'cause I'm not taking the final." She rose to retrieve it from the dresser, where it rested beneath the can of powder. "Remember to return it. Father always wants me to show him where he's spending his money, so I must take it home at semester break," she said sadly.

"What's this?" Huldah picked up the powder from where Emma had placed it next to a hairbrush. "I've heard of weird complexion treatments, but this is the limit!"

"I bought it for a friend," Rebecca answered defensively.

"Friends can be dangerous," Huldah snipped, "and a relationship like that could get explosive."

If looks were darts, Huldah would never have left Rebecca's room alive. Rebecca, however, soon forgot Huldah's teasing as she returned to her studies with Emma Jane.

Rebecca was relieved when the study session ended and the campus bell announced that the evening meal would be served in twenty minutes. Carefully wrapping the can of gunpowder in a brown paper sack, she slipped it into her coat pocket and quickly joined Emma Jane to walk to the dining hall, a spacious lounge and dining room in the lower level of the gymnasium.

Along a wall of the lounge were wooden pigeonholes which were receptacles for students' mail and such messages as faculty or friends might wish to pass on. Hurriedly ascertaining that Pug was not in the lounge, she quickly pushed the package into his box, then made a point of examining her own—empty except for a note from Miss Maxwell inviting her to a late tea after exams ended on Wednesday following.

7

THE TURKEY SHOOT

L ight snowflakes caught the sputter of the gaslights feebly illuminating the cobblestone walks which connected the brownstone-and-brick, ivy-entwined dormitories and academic buildings of Wareham Academy. Rebecca rather enjoyed the solitude of the walk to her dorm from Miss Emily Maxwell's apartment, her exams for the fall semester behind her. In only a few hours Thursday morning would arrive, and she would board the morning train to Riverboro depot with Emma Jane to spend a much-deserved long weekend with her aunts at the brick house.

Rebecca quickened her steps as she caught sight of a hurrying figure darting under a lamp in the tiny, triangular park that lay between the campus and the village. None of the crimes associated with city campuses had ever occurred at Wareham, but like all normal girls alone at night, Rebecca had no desire to meet a stranger in the dark.

The bell in the Wareham Academy library tower tolled eleven thirty as Rebecca entered the dorm that Wednesday evening. The evening hours at Miss Maxwell's apartment had passed quickly as she and two other girls—both upper-class students who lived off campus with their parents—had celebrated the end of another semester. She had intended to go straight to her room, but the door to Huldah Meserve's room popped open, and Huldah appeared, carrying a coffeepot. "Hi, Rebecca," she chirped, "care to join us?"

"It's late. I really musn't."

"No classes tomorrow, and the night is young."

Rebecca then spied Penelope Bennett and another of the Munjoy Hill girls sitting on a bed inside the open door. Her nose caught a faint odor of cigarette smoke, and tobacco, she knew, was strictly forbidden on the Wareham campus for students and faculty alike.

"I want to be fresh for my trip home. Good night," Rebecca said decidedly. As she mounted the steps to the second floor, Rebecca worried about what she had seen — or rather smelled. Not a tattler, she nevertheless did not wish to compromise either her convictions about smoking or the school's no-smoking policy. Besides, perhaps none of the girls had actually been smoking, she decided, wanting to believe the best. She remembered Emma Jane's embarrassment at returning from the barber shop smelling like a cigar smoker after having made the mistake of entering that masculine domain to get her hair trimmed.

Emma, not a night owl, was asleep when Rebecca tiptoed into their room. Without lighting the lamp, she quickly undressed, slipped into her flannel gown, and soon Rebecca was fast asleep.

Rebecca woke with a start, though she could not imagine the reason. Her dream of traveling by train to Riverboro had turned into a nightmare when the track in front of the hurtling locomotive erupted from a dynamite blast, and the train cars had tumbled end over end. She sat up in bed telling herself it must have been a bad scene from a cheap Western novel she had read recently, and that she must never read another one. Then she heard shrieks in the corridor.

Quickly she and Emma Jane joined a group of flannel-nightgowned girls at the large, plate-glass window at the end of the second-story hall. The glass in the top sash had unaccountably cracked from top to bottom. Across the campus Rebecca could see lamps begin to flicker in dorm windows, and in the gaslights she saw excited figures running through the snow toward the park, downhill from the campus toward Wareham Village.

Rebecca and Emma, now fully awake, decided to return to their room and dress to follow the excitement. Rebecca had pulled a dress over her nightgown and was pulling on her boots when there came a pounding at the door, then the door burst open. It was Huldah, and she was out of breath.

"Guess what, girls? Somebody fired the cannon — the one on the green! The whole town's up and about! It went off at midnight. Penny went out on the steps for some fresh air, and she heard it go off when the tower clock was striking twelve. The roar was so loud it made the sashes jump most out of their casements in the windows facing the village."

Rebecca laced her boots and walked down to the green. She moved with this group of girls and with that group; mostly she listened to the excited chatter about broken windows along Main Street. Seldom did she offer her comment. The entire town was out of bed, that soon was evident. Dogs were barking across the village, and the yapping of farmyard curs could be heard coming from well back into the hills above Wareham. Somewhere beyond the village a rooster crowed.

There was much disputation about how much damage had been done. Early reports were that the First Church steeple had been shot off. But the church sexton soon confirmed that the belfry was still as firmly attached as it had been when the edifice was erected before the Revolution. The chief damage seemed to be that several shop windows had been cracked.

It was after one in the morning when Rebecca returned to her bed. "It was two by the village clock," was a line from Longfellow's famous "Landlord's Tale" that echoed in her brain as the library tower bell tolled the hour of the night. Three o'clock struck. Four, and she "heard the bleating of the flock," as Paul Revere in the poem rode through the night to herald the coming of the British, as a harbinger of the Battle of Concord Bridge and the "shot heard round the world." "The British Regulars fired and fled," and Rebecca Randall tossed and turned unhappily in her bed.

Pug Wilson's can of gunpowder kept Rebecca awake that night long after the cannon's echo had died in the ears of her dorm mates. It filled what little sleep she did gain with visions of war, explosions, and cannon fire — always there were cannons — and Rebecca knew for certain that the war was not yet done.

She did not hear the clock strike five. Then Rebecca found herself shaken awake by Emma Jane. "Come on, Becky. Let's get our suitcases downstairs and go to breakfast. The train leaves at eight."

Rebecca and Emma Jane were polishing off the last of their hot hasty pudding when Miss Maxwell, worried and uncommonly agitated, demanded their presence at once in the principal's office. The girls followed Miss Maxwell to the faculty offices. Pug Wilson sat alone in the outer office, the picture of boredom, one foot resting on an empty chair. Principal Morrison's office was next, beyond a heavy oak door.

Mr. Morrison was stern, though not unkind. "I'll be brief," he said, clearing his throat. "The cannon on the green was fired last night, and such a prank was irresponsible, and dangerous as well. One of the cannon balls is missing. Who can tell where it might have landed, or how much damage it may have done, had it not cleared the church roof — taking a lightning rod with it, I might add."

"But, Mr. Morrison, surely you . . ."

He waved his hand, cutting off her explanation. "You were in your room when the gun went off. Two girls have told me that already. I'm sure Miss Perkins, your roommate, can attest to that also." Emma Jane nodded mechanically, too frightened to answer.

Rebecca felt the color climb hotly up her neck and cheeks. "And have those same two girls also told you I bought half a pound of gunpowder for Pug Wilson to hunt with?" she answered hotly. "Sir, I had nothing to do with the cannon."

In reply, Mr. Morrison slid a large, glossy photo from his desk drawer and pushed it across his desk toward Rebecca. She picked up the incriminating photo with trembling fingers. Plainly to be seen in her hand as she reclined on the cannon was the can with the words, "Black Powder — 8 oz." in bold letters.

Rebecca showed the photo briefly to Emma, then she passed it to Miss Maxwell. "Miss Maxwell, if my Aunt Miranda sees this photo, I'm finished at Wareham."

Mr. Morrison cleared his throat again. "Miss Randall," he intoned, "your career at Wareham is not contingent on whether or not your aunt sees the photo, I'm afraid."

"Mr. Morrison," put in Emily Maxwell, "it was nearly eleven thirty when Rebecca left my apartment, and by all accounts she was in her room before midnight when the cannon went off."

"And by all accounts, so was Pug Wilson — and anyone else I could even remotely suspect of involvement in this," explained Mr. Morrison. "It comes down to this — Wareham's fire chief is an old army artillery man, and he has assured me that that cannon could have been fired using a slow-burning fuse, lit as much as half an hour before it went off. So it's conceivable that the perpetrator was in his — or her — bed well before the excitement began."

"Sir . . . I . . . what can I say?" For the first time in her life, Rebecca was at a loss for words.

Mr. Morrison waved his hand. "So what we must ascertain," he rumbled on, "is not who was present when the gun went off, but who loaded the gun."

"Mr. Morrison," protested Miss Maxwell, "we have only circumstantial evidence. Can't we send these girls home and conduct our investigation during the holiday?"

"We could . . ." he opened his mouth to continue, but he was cut off by Emma Jane, who was suddenly taken by a brash fit of bravery.

"Mr. Morrison, I won't stand for it! If Becky gets expelled, I go, too! I *heard* Pug Wilson ask her to buy gunpowder for a turkey shoot — that's all. And so did a couple of other girls, and I'm sure a faculty member did too! I'll be back here tomorrow with my father and the governor and . . . and everybody in Riverboro if Rebecca gets kicked out!"

Principal Morrison teetered in his swivel chair, then he turned toward Miss Maxwell. "Turkey shoot?" He raised his querulous eyebrow.

"Some of the boys do hunt turkeys, Mr. Morrison. I'm sure you know they are permitted to bring their shotguns, so long as they are kept locked in the dean's closet."

"Yes, yes indeed," he answered thoughtfully.

By now Rebecca's wits had begun to clear. "Mr. Morrison, sir," she said carefully, "that's exactly what Pug said when he asked me to do him a favor and buy the gunpowder at the hardware store—that his gun was in the dean's closet and he needed the powder to hunt turkeys on Saturday."

"Who else heard him say that?"

"I heard him," Emma sang out.

Mr. Morrison shot a warning glance at Emma Jane.

"Emma Jane, for sure," said Rebecca. "And Mr. Archippus, the history teacher, was right on our heels. I'm sure he heard it."

Mr. Morrison stepped to an oak-and-nickel telephone mounted on the wall behind his desk. He turned the crank—one long ring and two short. Presently he spoke: "Dean Ashcroft, does Mr. Pug Wilson keep a shotgun in your closet?" Then after a pause, "I see. You've been very helpful."

Mr. Morrison then stepped into the outer office, returning quickly with Pug Wilson. "Sit down," he said evenly, motioning to a chair next to Emily Maxwell as he returned to his own seat behind the desk. "The word is out that you're quite a turkey hunter, Mr. Wilson."

"Well, yes, I like to hunt."

"You went last Saturday, then?"

"Well, er, no sir. Last Saturday I shot billiards at the Village Barber Shop."

"On the Saturday before exams? I've reviewed your grades, Wilson. You could better have used your time on the books. But do you own a shotgun?"

"Yes," Pug answered weakly.

"Where is it? Keep in mind that I've already spoken to Mr. Ashcroft about his practice of holding the boys' guns until they need them for hunting."

"It's . . ." Wilson looked briefly at the six hot, accusing eyes staring his direction. "It's in Portland. Actually, it's my father's. I don't hunt . . . that is, not very often."

"Then why did you need to order gunpowder from the hardware store?"

"I . . . I thought I'd have some fun."

"Rebecca and Emma, you may leave. Please accept my apologies for grilling you over this incident." Grimly Mr. Morrison passed Miss Maxwell the photo on his desk, and she slipped it to Rebecca who was quietly opening the door. "Do yourself and your aunts a favor and be sure this never reaches Riverboro," Emily Maxwell remarked. Her face was set as she spoke, but Rebecca imagined she caught a gleam in her eye.

"Thank you, sir," the girls answered in unison, though Mr. Morrison could not have heard them, for they were halfway across the outer office by the time the words escaped their lips. Mere seconds later they had their bags and were running toward the depot, where the train was already taking on passengers as the locomotive hissed angrily in the still, sharp air of a frigid northern January morning.

"I feel like a fool, letting Pug Wilson trick me into buying that gunpowder," Rebecca spouted to Emma later on the car, as she ripped the photo into tiny pieces and stuffed it into an ashtray.

"Join the world of real people," Emma chortled coyly. "Many's the time *I've* felt the fool when *you* seemed so clever." Together, Emma Jane and Rebecca laughed uncontrollably until Huldah Meserve, sulking by herself in the other end of the railway car, could stand it no longer.

"Let me in on your merry little secret or I shall surely die of curiosity," Huldah said, seating herself across the aisle from them.

"Munjoy Hill is a great place to hunt turkeys," was all Rebecca would say. Huldah stormed off as the girls continued their fit of the giggles.

8

THE LITTLE PROPHET

I guess York County will never get rid of that thievin'
Simpson crew!" exclaimed Miranda Sawyer to her sister Jane one July morning after Rebecca's first year at
Wareham. "I thought when the family moved to Acreville
we'd seen the last of 'em, but we ain't! The big, cross-
eyed, stutterin' boy has got a job at the sawmill in Maplewood. That's near enough to come over to Riverboro once
in a while on a Sunday mornin' and set in the meetin'
house starin' at Rebecca same as he used to do, only it's
riskier now both of 'em are older. Then Mrs. Fogg goes
and brings back the biggest Simpson girl to help her take
care of her baby — as if there wa'n't plenty of help nearer
home! Now I hear say that the younger twin has come to
stay the summer with the Gileses that live over by the
meetin' house."

"I thought twins were always the same age," said Rebecca with mild amusement, as she came into the kitchen
carrying a pail of milk from Robinson's barn.

"So they be," snapped Miranda, flushing and correcting herself. "But that pasty-faced Simpson twin looks
younger and is smaller than the other one. He's meek as
Moses, and the other one is as bold as a brass kettle. I

81

don't see how they come to be twins—they ain't a mite
alike."

"Elijah was always called the 'fighting twin' at
school," remembered Rebecca, "and Elisha's nickname
was Namby Pamby. But I think he's a nice boy, and I'm
glad he has come back. He won't like living with Mr.
Giles, but he'll be almost next door to the minister's, and
Mrs. Baxter is sure to hire him to weed her garden."

The "Simpson crew" were the children of Abner Simpson, and his habit of stealing property which Riverboro
householders failed to keep locked up had earned him several terms locked up in the York County Jail. During the
last of his incarcerations, Riverboro's municipal officers—
the selectmen and the constable—took it upon themselves
to move the Simpson family to Acreville, across the
county line to the town of their birth.

"I wonder why the boy's stayin' with Parker Giles,"
said Jane. "To be sure they haven't got any children of
their own, but the child's too young to be of much use."

"I know why," remarked Rebecca promptly, "for I
heard all about it over to Robinson's barn when I was getting the milk. Mr. Giles traded something with Abner
Simpson two years ago and got the best of the bargain,
and Mr. Robinson says he heard over at the store he's the
only man that ever did, and he ought to have a monument
put up to him. So Mr. Giles owes Mr. Simpson money,
and he won't pay it. And Mr. Simpson said he'd send over
a child and board part of it out, and take the rest in
stock—a pig or a calf or something."

"That's all stuff and nonsense," exclaimed Miranda.
"Nothin' in the world but men-talk. You git a clump of
menfolks settin' round the stove in Watson's Mercantile,
or out on the bench at the door, an' they'll make up stories
as fast as their tongues can wag. The man don't live that's

smart enough to cheat Abner Simpson in a trade, and who ever heard of anybody owin' him money? Tain't supposable that a woman like Mrs. Giles would allow her husband to be in debt to a man like Abner Simpson. It's a sight likelier that she heard that Mrs. Simpson was ailin' and sent for the boy so as to help the family along. She always had Mrs. Simpson to do her laundry for her once a month, if you remember, Jane?"

Parker Giles was a close man, close of mouth and close of purse. And all that Riverboro ever knew as to the three months' visit of the Simpson twin was that it actually occurred. Elisha, otherwise Namby Pamby, came; Namby Pamby stayed; and Namby Pamby, when he finally rejoined his own domestic circle, did not go empty-handed, for he was accompanied on his homeward travels by a large, red, bony, somewhat mean-dispositioned cow, who was tied on behind the wagon and who made the journey a lively and eventful one by her total lack of desire to proceed over the road from Riverboro to Acreville. But the cow's tale belongs to another time and place, and the coward's tale must come first, for Elisha Simpson was held to be sadly lacking in the manly quality of courage.

It was the minister's wife, Mrs. Baxter, who called Namby Pamby the Little Prophet. His full name was Elisha Jeremiah Simpson, but one seldom heard it at full length, since if he escaped the ignominy of being called Namby Pamby, Lisha was quite enough for an urchin just in his first long trousers. He was "Lisha," therefore, to the village, but the Little Prophet to the young minister's wife.

Rebecca could see the Giles' brown farmhouse from Mrs. Baxter's sitting-room window when she had gone there to be tutored in her Latin or French. Its little-traveled lane with strips of tufted green between the wheel tracks curled dustily up to the very doorstep. And inside the screen door of pink copper mosquito netting was a wonderful drawn-in rug shaped like a half pie, with "Welcome" in saffron letters on a green ground.

Rebecca liked Mrs. Cora Giles, who was a friend of her Aunt Miranda's and one of the few persons who exchanged calls with that somewhat unsociable lady. The Giles farm was not a long walk from the brick house, for Rebecca could go across the fields when haying time was over. Her delight at being sent on an errand in that direction could not be measured, now that the minister and his wife had grown to be such a resource in her life. She liked to see Mrs. Giles shake the Welcome rug, flinging the cheery word out into the summer sunshine like a bright greeting to the day. She liked to see her come to the screen door a dozen times in a morning, open it a crack and chase an imaginary fly from the sacred precincts within. She liked to see her come up the cellar steps into the side garden, appearing mysteriously as from the bowels of the earth, carrying a shining pan of milk in both hands, and disappearing through the beds of hollyhocks and sunflowers to the pigpen or the henhouse.

Rebecca was not fond of Parker Giles and neither was Mrs. Baxter, nor Elisha, for that matter. In fact, Mr. Giles was rather a difficult person to grow fond of, with his fiery red beard, his freckled skin, and his gruff way of speaking. There had been no children in the brown house to smooth the creases from his forehead or the roughness from his voice.

The new minister's wife was sitting in her porch glider under the shade of her great maple early one morning when she first saw the Little Prophet. A tiny figure came down the grass-grown road leading a cow by a rope. If it had been a small boy and a small cow, a middle-sized boy and an ordinary cow, or a grown man and a big cow, she

*A tiny figure came down the grass-grown road
leading a cow by a rope.*

might not have noticed them. But it was the combination of an insignificant boy and a huge cow that attracted her attention. She could not guess the child's years, she only knew that he was small for his age, whatever it was.

The cow was a dark red beast with a crumpled horn, a white star on her forehead, and a large, surprised sort of eye. She had, of course, two eyes, and both were surprised, but the left one had an added hint of amazement in it by virtue of a few white hairs lurking accidentally in the center of the eyebrow.

The boy had a thin, sensitive face and curly brown hair, trousers patched on both knees, and a ragged straw hat on the back of his head. Sometimes he pattered along behind the cow, holding the rope with both hands and getting over the ground in a jerky way, stubbing his toes bloody on stones as he went since the animal left him no time to think of a smooth path for bare feet. Sometimes he raced ahead, keeping the length of frayed rope between him and the cow, in terror that the cow *would* decide to hurry and hook him with her one good horn.

The Giles pasture was a good half-mile distant, and the cow seemed in no hurry to reach it. Accordingly she forsook the road now and then and rambled in the hollows, where to her way of thinking the grass was sweeter. She started on one of these exploring expeditions just as she passed the minister's spreading maple tree, which gave Mrs. Baxter time to call out to the little fellow, "Is that your cow?"

Elisha blushed and smiled and tried to speak modestly, but there was a quiver of pride in his voice as he answered suggestively, "It's . . . nearly my cow."

"How is that?" asked Mrs. Baxter.

"Why, Mr. Giles says when I drive her twenty-nine more times to pasture 'thout her gettin' her foot over the rope or 'thout my bein' afraid, she's goin' to be my truly cow. Are you 'fraid of cows?"

"Ye-e-es," Mrs. Baxter confessed, "I am, just a little. You see, I am a city girl who has come to live in the country, and country boys can't understand how city girls feel about cows."

"I can! They're awful big things, aren't they?"

"Perfectly enormous! I've always thought a cow coming toward you to be one of the biggest things in the world."

"Yes! Me, too. Don't let's think about it. Do they hook people so very often?"

"I'm not sure, child. But I've never heard of one hooking," she assured him quickly.

"If they stepped on your bare foot they'd scrunch it, wouldn't they?"

"Yes, but you are the driver. You mustn't let them do that. You are a free-will boy, and they are nothing but cows."

"I know. But p'r'aps there are free-will cows, and if they just *would* do it you couldn't help being scrunched, for you mustn't let go of the rope nor run, Mr. Giles says."

"No, of course, that would never do, I'm sure," Mrs. Baxter agreed.

"Where you used to live did all the cows go down into the boggy places when you drove 'em to pasture, or did some walk in the road?"

"There weren't any cows or any pastures where I used to live. That's what makes me so foolish. Why does your cow need a rope?"

"She don't like to go to pasture, Mr. Giles says. Sometimes she'd druther stay to home, and so when she gets part way she turns 'round and comes backwards."

Dear me! thought Mrs. Baxter, *what becomes of this boy-mite if the cow has a spell of going backwards?* "Do you like to drive her?" she asked.

"N-no, not erzackly. But, you see, it'll be my cow if I drive her twenty-nine more times 'thout her gettin' her foot over the rope and 'thout my bein' afraid." A beaming smile gave a passing brightness to his harassed little face. "Will she feed in the ditch much longer?" he asked. "Shall I say 'Hurrap'? That's what Mr. Giles says—*Hurrap* like that, and it means to hurry up."

It was a rather feeble warning that he sounded, and the cow fed on peacefully. The little fellow looked up at the minister's wife confidingly, and then glanced back at the farm to see if Parker Giles were watching the progress of events.

"What shall we do next?" he asked.

Mrs. Baxter delighted in that warm, cosy little *we.* It took her into the conversation so pleasantly. She was weak, indeed, when it came to cows, but all the courage in her soul rose to arms when Elisha said, "What shall *we* do next?" She became alert, ingenious, strong, on the instant.

"What is the cow's name?" she asked, sitting up straight in her porch glider.

"Buttercup. But she don't seem to know it very well. She ain't a mite like a buttercup."

"Never mind. You must shout 'Buttercup!' at the top of your voice and twitch the rope *hard.* Then I'll call, 'Hurrap!' with all my might at the same moment. And if she starts quickly, we mustn't run nor seem frightened!"

They did this. It worked like a charm, and Mrs. Baxter watched her Little Prophet affectionately as the cow pulled him down Tory Hill.

The lovely summer days wore on. Rebecca was often at the parsonage and saw Elisha frequently, but Buttercup was seldom present during her visits, as the boy now drove her to the pasture very early in the morning.

Mr. Giles had pointed out the necessity of getting her into the pasture at least a few minutes before she had to be taken out again at night, and though Rebecca didn't like Mr. Giles, she saw the common sense of this remark. Sometimes Mrs. Baxter caught a glimpse of the two at sundown as they returned from the pasture to the twilight milking, Buttercup chewing her peaceful cud, her soft white bag of milk hanging full, her surprised eye rolling in its accustomed frenzy. The frenzied roll did not mean anything, they used to assure Elisha. But if it didn't, it was an awful pity she had to do it, Rebecca thought, and Mrs. Baxter agreed. To have an expression of eye that meant murder, and yet to be a perfectly gentle and well-meaning animal — this was a calamity indeed.

Mrs. Baxter was looking at the sun one evening as it dropped like a ball of fire beyond the White Mountains when the Little Prophet passed. "It's the twenty-ninth night," he called joyously.

"I am so glad," she answered, for she had often feared some accident might prevent his claiming the promised reward. "Then tomorrow Buttercup will be your own cow?"

"I guess so. That's what Mr. Giles said. He's off to Acreville now, but he'll be home tonight, and Father's going to send my new hat by him. When Buttercup's my own cow, I wish I could change her name and call her Red Rover, but p'r'aps her mother wouldn't like it. When she b'longs to me, mebbe I won't be so 'fraid of gettin' hooked and scrunched, because she'll know she's mine, and she'll go better. I haven't let her get snarled up in the rope one single time, and I don't show I'm afraid, do I?"

"I should never suspect it for an instant," said Mrs. Baxter encouragingly. "I've often envied you and your bold, brave look!"

Elisha appeared distinctly pleased. "I haven't cried, either, when she's dragged me over the pasture bars and peeled my legs. Wilbur Potter's little brother, Charlie, says he ain't afraid of anything, not even bears. He says he would walk right up close and cuff 'em if they dared to yip. But I ain't like that! He ain't scared of elephants or tigers or lions either. He says they're all the same as frogs or chickens to him!"

Rebecca told her Aunt Miranda that evening that it was the Prophet's twenty-ninth night, and that the big red cow was to be his on the morrow.

"Well, I hope it'll turn out that way," she said. "But I ain't a mite sure that Parker Giles will give up that cow when it comes to the point. It won't be the first time he's tried to crawl out of a bargain with folks a good deal bigger than Lisha, for he's terrible close, Parker is. To be sure, he's stiff in his joints, and he's glad enough to have a boy to take the cow to the pasture in summertime, but he always has hired help when it comes harvestin'. So Lisha'll be no use from this on, and I dare say the cow is Abner Simpson's anyway. If you want a walk tonight, I wish you'd go up there and ask Miz Giles if she'll lend me an' your Aunt Jane half a yeast cake. Tell her we'll pay it back when we get ours Saturday. Don't you want to take Thirza Meserve with you? She's alone as usual while Huldah's entertainin' a boy on the side porch. Don't stay too long at the parsonage!"

9

PARKER GILES'S BARGAIN

R ebecca was used to being sent on this sort of errand by her aunts, for the whole village of Riverboro would sometimes be rocked to the very center of its being by simultaneous desire for a yeast cake. As the yeast cakes were valued at two cents and wouldn't keep—the demand being uncertain and dependent entirely on a fluctuating desire for "riz bread"—the storekeeper refused to order more than three yeast cakes a day at his own risk. Sometimes eight or ten persons would hitch up their teams and drive from distant farms for the coveted article only to be met with Watson's flat, "No, I'm all out of yeast cake. Miz Simmons took the last. Mebbe you can borry half o' hern. She hain't much of a bread eater."

So Rebecca climbed the hill to Mrs. Giles's knowing that her daily bread depended on her returning with a yeast cake. Thirza Meserve trotted alongside Rebecca barefooted, and tough as her little feet were, the long walk over the stubble fields tired her. When they came within sight of the Giles's barn, she coaxed Rebecca to take a shortcut through the turnips growing in long, beautifully weeded rows.

"You know Mr. Giles is awfully cross, Thirza, and he can't bear anybody to tread on his crops or touch a tree or a bush that belongs to him. I'm kind of nervous about it. But come along and mind that you step softly in between the rows and hold up your petticoat, so you can't possibly touch the turnip plants. I'll do the same. Skip along fast, because then we won't leave any deep footprints."

Rebecca and little Thirza passed safely and noiselessly along, their pleasure a trifle enhanced by the felt dangers of their progress. Rebecca knew that they were doing no harm, but that did not prevent her hoping to escape the beady eye of Mr. Giles.

As they neared the outer edge of the turnip patch, girl and child paused suddenly, petticoats in the air. A great clump of elderberry bushes hid them from the barn, but from the other side of the clump came the sound of conversation — the timid voice of the Little Prophet and the gruff tones of Parker Giles.

Rebecca was afraid to interrupt and too honest to wish to overhear. She could only hope the man and the boy would pass on to the house as they talked, so she motioned to the paralyzed Thirza to take two more steps and stand with her behind the elderberry bushes. But no! In a moment they heard Mr. Giles drag a stool over beside the grindstone.

"Well, now, Elisha Jeremiah," Mr. Giles said, "we'll talk about the red cow. You say you've drove her a month, do ye, and the trade between us was that if you could drive her a month without her getting the rope over her foot and without bein' afraid, you was to have her. That's straight, ain't it?"

The Prophet's face burned with excitement, his gingham shirt rose and fell as if he were breathing hard, but he only nodded assent and said nothing.

"Now," continued Mr. Giles, "have you made out to keep the rope from under her feet?"

"She ain't got t-t-tangled up one s-single time," said Elisha, stuttering in his excitement but looking up with some courage from his bare toes, with which he was busily threading the grass.

"So far, so good. Now 'bout bein' afraid. As you seem so certain of gettin' the cow, I suppose you hain't been a speck scared, hev you? Honor bright, now!"

"I . . . I . . . not but just a little mite. I . . ."

"Hold up a minute. Of course, you didn't *say* you was afraid, you didn't *show* you was afraid, and nobody knew you *was* afraid, but that ain't the way we fixed it up. You was to call the cow your'n if you could drive her to the pasture for a month without *bein'* afraid. Own up square, now. Hev you been afraid?"

A long pause, then a faint, "Yes."

"Where's your manners?"

"I mean, yes, sir."

"How often? If it hain't been too many times, mebbe I'll let ye off, though you're a reg'lar girl-boy, and you'll be runnin' away from the cat bimeby. Has it been . . . twice?"

"Yes," and the Little Prophet's voice was very faint now, and it had a decided tear in it.

"Yes what?"

"Yes, sir."

"Has it been four times?"

"Y-es, sir." More heaving of the gingham shirt.

"Well, you *air* a thunderin' coward! How many times? Speak up now."

More digging of the bare toes in the earth, and one premonitory teardrop stealing from under the downcast lids, then . . .

"A little, most every day, and you can keep the cow," wailed the Prophet, as he turned abruptly and fled behind the shed where he flung himself into the green depths of a rhubarb bed and gave himself up to unmanly sobs.

Parker Giles gave a sort of shamefaced guffaw at the abrupt departure of the boy. He went on into the house, while Rebecca and Thirza stealthily circled the barn and politely entered the parsonage front gate.

Rebecca told the minister's wife what she could remember of the interview between Mr. Giles and Elisha Simpson. Tenderhearted Mrs. Baxter longed to seek and comfort her Little Prophet sobbing in the rhubarb bed, the brand of coward on his forehead, and what was much worse, the fear in his heart that he deserved it.

Rebecca could hardly be prevented from bearding Mr. Giles and openly demanding justice for the cause of Elisha, for she was an impetuous, reckless, valiant young lady when a weaker vessel was attacked or threatened unjustly.

Mrs. Baxter acknowledged that Mr. Giles had been true in a way to his word and bargain, but she stated also that she had never heard of so cruel and hard a bargain since the days of Shylock, and it was all the worse for being made with a child.

Rebecca hurried home, her visit quite spoiled and her errand quite forgotten till she reached the brick house door, where she told her aunts that she would rather eat buttermilk bread till she died than partake of food mixed with one of the Giles's yeast cakes—that it would choke her, even in the shape of good raised bread.

"That's all very fine, Rebecca," said her Aunt Miranda, who had a pinprick for almost every bubble. "But don't forget there's two other mouths to feed in this house, and you might at least give your Aunt Jane and me the privilege of chokin' if we feel to want to!"

10

THE LITTLE PROPHET PULLS A TURNIP

Mrs. Baxter finally heard from Cora Giles, through whom all information was sure to filter if you gave it time, that her husband despised a coward, that he considered Elisha a regular mother's-apron-string boy, and that he was "learnin' him to be brave."

Wilbur Potter, the hired man, now drove Buttercup to pasture, though whenever Mr. Giles went to town, as he often did, Mrs. Baxter noticed that Elisha took the hired man's place. She often joined him on these anxious expeditions, and a like terror in both their souls, they attempted to train the red cow and give her some idea of obedience.

"If she only wouldn't look at us that way, we would get along real nicely with her, wouldn't we?" prattled the Prophet, straggling along by her side. "And she is a splendid cow. She gives twenty-one quarts a day, and Mr. Giles says it's more'n half cream."

The minister's wife assented to all this, thinking that if Buttercup would give up her habit of turning completely round in the road to roll her eyes and elevate her white-tipped eyebrow, she might indeed be an enjoyable companion. But in her present state of training, her company was not enjoyable even when she did give sixty-one quarts of milk a day. Furthermore, when Mrs. Baxter discovered that she never did any of these troublesome things with Wilbur Potter, she began to believe cows to be more intelligent creatures than she had supposed, and she was indignant to think that Buttercup could count so confidently on the weakness of a small boy and a timid woman.

One evening, when Buttercup was more than usually exasperating, Mrs. Baxter said to the Prophet, who was bracing himself to keep from being pulled into a wayside brook where Buttercup loved to dabble, "Elisha, do you know anything about the superiority of mind over matter?"

No, he didn't, though it was not a fair time to ask the question, for he had sat down in the road to get a better grip on the rope.

"Give me that rope. I can pull like an ox in my present frame of mind. You run down on the opposite side of the brook, take that big stick, wade right in — you are barefooted — brandish the stick, and if necessary clobber that cow! I would go myself, but it is better she should recognize you as her master, and I am in as much danger as you are, anyway. She may try to hook you, but you must keep waving the stick. Die brandishing, Prophet, that's the idea! She may turn and run after me. I shall run, too, but I shall die running, and the minister can bury us under our favorite sweet apple tree!"

The Prophet's soul was fired by the lovely lady's speech. Their spirits mounted together, and they were filled with a splendid courage in which death looked a mean and paltry thing compared with conquering that cow. She had already stepped into the pool, but the Prophet waded in toward her, moving his alder club menacingly. She looked up with the familiar roll of the eye that had done her such good service all summer, but she quivered beneath the stern justice and the new valor of the Prophet's gaze.

In that moment perhaps she felt ashamed of the misery she had caused the helpless little boy. At any rate, she turned and walked back into the road, leaving the boy and the lady rather disappointed at their easy victory. To be prepared for a violent death and receive not even a scratch made them fear that they might possibly have overestimated the danger.

They were better friends than ever after that, the young minister's wife and the forlorn little boy from Acreville, sent away from home he knew not why, unless it were that there was little to eat at home and considerably more at the Giles's.

Summer grew into autumn, and the minister's great maple flung a flaming bough of scarlet over Mrs. Baxter's porch glider where it reposed on the slate flagstones. Parker Giles found Elisha very useful at digging up potatoes and picking apples, but the boy was going back to his family as soon as the harvesting was over.

One Friday evening Mrs. Baxter and Rebecca, wrapped in shawls and sweaters, were sitting on the parsonage front steps enjoying the sunset. Rebecca was in a tremulous state of happiness, for she had come directly from the Academy at Wareham to the parsonage, and as the minister was absent at a church conference, she was to stay the night with Mrs. Baxter and go with her to Portland the next day.

Not only was this Rebecca's first visit to a city, but they were to go by ferry to the islands of Casco Bay, eat lunch in a restaurant, ride a trolley car, and visit the Longfellow house—all of which were entirely new experiences for Rebecca, though city-bred girls would surely have marveled at her excitement. Rebecca in her happiness radiated flashes and sparkles of joy, making Mrs. Baxter wonder if flesh could be translucent, enabling the fires of the spirit and soul to shine through the body.

Buttercup was being milked by the hired man on the grassy slope near Giles's shed door just up the way from the parsonage. As she walked to the barn after giving up her yellow milk, she bent her neck and snatched a hasty bite from a pile of turnips lying temptingly near. In her haste she took more of a mouthful than would be considered good manners, even among cows, and as she disappeared through the barn door they could see a forest of green tops hanging from her mouth while she painfully attempted to grind up the mass of stolen vegetables without allowing a single turnip to escape.

It grew dark soon afterward, and Mrs. Baxter and Rebecca went over to the Giles's house to see Mrs. Giles's new lamp lighted for the first time, to examine her latest drawn-in rug—a wonderful achievement produced entirely from dyed flannel petticoats—and to hear the doctor's wife, who was also visiting, play "Oft in the Stilly Night" on the piano.

As they closed the sitting room door opening on the piazza facing the barn, the women heard the cow coughing and said to one another, "Buttercup was too greedy and now she has indigestion."

Elisha always went to bed at sundown, and Parker Giles had gone to the doctor's to have his hand bandaged, for he had hurt it in the threshing machine. Wilbur Potter came in presently and asked for him, saying that the cow coughed more and more, and it must be that something was wrong, but he could not get her to open her mouth wide enough for him to see anything. "She'd up an' die ruther 'n oblige anybody, that infernal ugly cow would!" he said.

When Mr. Giles had driven into the yard, he came in for a lantern and went directly out to the barn without stopping to unhitch his horse. After a half-hour or so, in which the little party of women had forgotten the whole occurrence, he came in again.

"I'm blamed if we ain't goin' to lose that cow," he said. "Come out, will ye, Cora, and hold the lantern. I can't do anything with my right hand in a sling, and Will is the stupidest critter in the country."

Giles and his wife hurried out to the barn, and the doctor's wife drove off to her house to see if her brother Moses had come home from Milltown and could come and take a hand in the emergency. Rebecca and Mrs. Baxter, catching the excitement from the shouting and hurrying and scurrying about, slipped quietly into Giles's barn to see for themselves what was going on.

Buttercup was in a bad way; there was no doubt about it. One of the turnips had lodged in her throat, and it would move neither way despite her attempts to dislodge it. Her breathing was labored, and her eyes were bloodshot from straining and choking. Once or twice they succeeded in getting her mouth partly open, but before they could discover the cause of her trouble she had wrested her head away.

"I can see a little tuft of green sticking straight up in the middle," said Parker, while Wilbur held a lantern above Buttercup's head. "But land, it's so far down, and such a mite of a thing, I couldn't git it even if I could use my right hand. S'pose you try Will."

Wilbur hemmed and hawed and confessed he didn't care to try. Buttercup's grinders were of good size and excellent quality, and he had no fancy for leaving his hand within her jaws. He said he was no good at that kind of work, but that he would help Parker hold the cow's head. That was just as necessary and considerably safer, he decided.

Moses, who by now had arrived with his sister in her buggy, agreed to give his best shot at retrieving the recalcitrant turnip, while Will restrained Buttercup and Giles held the lantern. He did his best, wrapping his wrist in a cloth and making desperate but ineffectual dabs at the slippery green turnip tops in the reluctantly opened throat. The cow tossed her head and stamped her feet and switched her tail and wriggled from under Will's hands, so that it seemed altogether impossible to reach the seat of trouble.

Giles was in despair, fuming and fretting the more because of his own crippled hand.

"Cora," he said, "you drive over to North Riverboro for the veterinarian. I know we can git out that turnip if we can hit on the right tools and somebody to manage 'em right. But we've got to be quick about it, or the critter'll choke to death sure! Your hand's so clumsy, Mose, she thinks her time's come when she feels it in her mouth, and your fingers are so big you can't ketch holt o' that green stuff 'thout its slippin'!"

"Mine ain't big. Let me try," said a timid voice, and turning around, they saw little Elisha Simpson, his trousers pulled on over his nightshirt, his curly hair ruffled, his eyes vague with sleep.

Parker Giles gave a laugh of good-humored derision. "You—that's afraid to drive a cow to pasture? Nosuh! You hain't got spine enough for this job, I guess!"

Buttercup just then gave a worse cough than ever, and her eyes rolled in her head as if she were giving up the ghost. "I'd rather do it than see her choke to death!" cried the boy, in despair.

"Then by ginger, you can try it, sonny!" said Giles. "Now this time we'll tie her head up. Take it slow and make a good job of it."

They pried poor Buttercup's jaws open to put a wooden gag between them, tied her head up, and kept her as still as they could while the women held the lanterns.

"Now, sonny, strip up your sleeve and reach as fur down's you can! Wind your little fingers in among that green stuff stickin' up there, give it a twist, and pull for all you're worth. Land! What a skinny little pipe stem!"

The Little Prophet had stripped up his sleeve. It was a slender thing, his arm. But he had driven the red cow all summer, borne her tantrums, protected her from the consequences of her own obstinacy, taking a future owner's pride in her splendid flow of milk—grown fond of her, in a word, and now she was choking to death. A skinny little pipe stem is capable of a great deal at such a time, and only a slender hand and arm could have done the work.

Elisha trembled, but encouraged by Mrs. Baxter, he made a dexterous and dashing entrance into the awful cavern of Buttercup's mouth. He descended upon the tiny clump of green turnip tops, wound his little fingers in among them as firmly as he could, and then gave a long, steady, determined pull with all the strength in his body. That was not so much in itself, to be sure, but he borrowed a good deal more energy from some reserve, the location of which nobody knows anything about, but upon which everybody draws in time of need.

Such a valiant pull you would never have expected of the Little Prophet. Such a pull it was that, to his own utter amazement, he suddenly found himself lying flat on his back on the barn floor with a very slippery something in his hand and a fair-sized but rather dilapidated turnip at the end of it.

"That's the business!" cried Moses.

"I could 'a' done it as easy as nothin' if my arm had been a leetle mite smaller," said Will Potter.

"You're a trump, sonny!" exclaimed Parker Giles, as he helped Moses untie Buttercup's head and took the gag out. "You're a trump, Lisha, and by ginger, the cow's your'n. Only don't you let your blessed pa drink none of her cream!"

The welcome air rushed into Buttercup's lungs and cooled her parched, torn throat. She was pretty nearly spent, poor thing, and she bent her head over the Little Prophet's shoulder as he threw his arms joyfully about her neck and whispered, "You're my truly cow now, ain't you, Buttercup?"

"Mrs. Baxter, dear," said Rebecca, as they walked back to the parsonage together under the young harvest moon, "there are all sorts of cowards, aren't there, and don't you think Elisha is one of the best kind."

"I don't quite know what to think about cowards, Rebecca," said the minister's wife hesitatingly. "The Little Prophet is the third coward I have known in my short life who turned out to be a hero when the real testing time came. Meanwhile the heroes themselves — or the ones who were thought heroes — were always busy doing something or being somewhere else."

11

ABIJAH FLAGG'S EDUCATION

A bijah Flagg was uneducable. That was the consensus of the Riverboro District School Committee. His father, a hard-drinking n'er-do-well drifter, had been found floating in the mill pond when Abijah was twelve. This, at least, lent a certain stability to Abijah's life, for instead of following Percy Flagg from job to job, from county to county, with each seasonal employment, he and his mother, Abbie, found themselves more or less permanently settled as paupers on Riverboro's town farm.

Abijah was then enrolled against his will in the village school. His career as a scholar lasted less than a month, and it ended abruptly for reasons having little to do with education. Abijah proved to be a leader, though not the kind who endears himself to young schoolmarms struggling to keep order and educate at the same time. Since lanky Abijah was big for his age, his teacher, Miss Dearborn, a resourceful young lass of seventeen, decided to give him the task of tending the fire in the school's pot-bellied stove.

An early cold spell in September required a morning fire for several consecutive damp days late in the month. Then, on a Thursday afternoon, Miss Dearborn said, "'Bijah, there's a chill moving in on the north wind tonight. It's a full moon, and there'll be a hard frost tomorrow morning for sure. Can you be over here at seven o'clock to get the stove goin' well before school?"

"Sure thing, Miss Dearborn." And Abijah was on his way home.

When Miss Dearborn arrived with the rest of her scholars at eight on Friday, Abijah was nowhere to be seen. But a gratifying curl of smoke from the chimney told them that he had done his duty.

She opened the door—and retreated gasping and coughing. Abijah had started the fire, all right. He had stuffed the stove full of green boughs and needles from the lonesome pine in the schoolyard. With the draft wide open and the damper closed, the stove had turned the one-room school into such a smokehouse that Alice Robinson's father could have smoked his bacon in there. It became Miss Dearborn's unhappy duty to cover her face with a damp kerchief and crawl on hands and knees to the stove in the center of the room to open the damper—letting the acrid fumes up the chimney—then close the draft to corral the roaring fire. The rest of the forenoon the windows were open to air out the school.

Abijah never returned to school as a scholar after this. Later, when Miss Dearborn let the school committee review the progress of his brief flirt with education, they agreed with her that it was best for all concerned if he stayed home.

Just before Christmas, Abijah's mother, who had been ailing since her common-law husband had drowned, passed on, struck down by consumption—tuberculosis to modern readers. Though Abijah had shared her lonely room at the poor farm, a small attic cubicle where she had been banished to protect the other inmates from her constant coughing and spitting, when the doctor later examined Abijah with his stethoscope he declared him free of TB and healthy enough to mingle with society.

"Say, Bill," said Squire Bean to Mr. Perkins the following April, as he waited in Perkins's blacksmith shop to get a new colter made for his steel plow, "I need a boy beginning next month to cut up my seed potatoes and help me plant 'em, too, probably. Isn't there a kid over to the poor farm just idling—the boy who was kicked out of school for smoking it up?"

Bill Perkins, who was Riverboro's first selectman and overseer of the poor, assented that this was true.

"Mrs. Bean and I could give the boy a good home—if he's a-mind to work. We don't have a child of our own, not even a grown one. Since our Samuel died years ago, Martha's been kind of lonesome."

"He's a skinny youngun, that Abijah Flagg," commented the practical Perkins. "Tall as a gatepost and thin as one, too. He's hungry all the time—threatens to eat the poor farm's larder up all by himself. Sure you kin manage 'im?"

"Martha can certainly fatten him up," said the squire, mindful of his own more-than-ample girth. "'Course we don't have much left in the cellar but last year's potatoes and a few shelves of canned goods until this year's garden comes in," he added with a chuckle. "But our hens are starting to lay pretty good, so I imagine we'll have enough and to spare for a boy for a while. Cow's milkin' good, too. And I reckon Watson's Mercantile can sell us what groceries we lack," he said. "An extra hand would make a sight of difference on my farm."

Selectman Perkins assented that the squire was no doubt right. Perkins knew the squire's circumstances — a retired lawyer with money enough to give a child a good home — and he had no compunctions about giving Abijah away at once, relieving the drain on the tax load at the poor farm.

"Tell ye what. We've got a selectmen's meetin' comin' up next week. I'll bring it up. My feelin' is, you've got yerself a boy fer plantin' season — mebbe longer, if you and he can get along."

And that is how Abijah Flagg came to be Squire Bean's chore boy — and eventually his heir. Of the squire's 160-acre hardscrabble farm, which he had purchased more for its picturesque view of the Saco River and the White Mountains beyond than for its agricultural potential, Abijah Flagg once said that were he to sell it off, stock and all, after the squire's decease, he couldn't raise more than a month's wages from the proceeds to compensate for all the years he had labored on that rocky hillside place.

&a &a &a

"What're we workin' on today, Becky?" Abijah Flagg pitched several forkfuls of yelloweye bean vines onto a canvas spread on Squire Bean's barn floor as he spoke. It was the middle of a glorious Saturday morning in October, and Rebecca, Latin book in hand, had climbed the long hill to the Bean farm as soon as the breakfast dishes were done in the brick house. For most youngsters in Riverboro, Saturday was a holiday. But for Abijah, it was the only day for school — the day in which he could practice with Rebecca that which he had studied all week during long evening hours at his table with his coal-oil lamp in the shed chamber. For Rebecca, now a student at Wareham

Academy, had found that the time she could spend tutoring Abijah was now limited indeed.

"Caesar," Rebecca chirped. "How about if I give you the English and you translate it back into Latin?"

"Fire away, Becky!" he said as he picked up his flail to thresh out the dried beans. This was the kind of exercise Abijah enjoyed—physical and mental work at the same time. He could translate Latin into English easily enough, guessing at the verb tenses by the context. Since one language seldom translates into another exactly, getting a close proximity would usually do, even for the most fastidious teacher. But to put English back into Latin required an exact knowledge of the dead tongue's tenses and mode. Abijah *had* to learn Latin in order to do so—or he would need to memorize the book! He found exhilarating the challenge of beating Rebecca at her own game.

"Let's try *Book Three* of Caesar's *Commentaries* on his war in Gaul, section fourteen," Rebecca said gravely. She read:

> After taking many of their towns, Caesar, perceiving that so much labor was wasted, and that the flight of the enemy could not be prevented, and that he could not injure them, he determined to wait for his fleet.

"Whoa, hold it," Abijah said, taking an enthusiastic swing with his flail. "That's all I can digest at a lick." He began to translate:

> *Compluribus expugnatis oppidis, Caesar, abi intellixit frustra tantum laborem sumi, . . .*

"That's all right!" chuckled Rebecca, who had a Latin/English translation open before her, "I couldn't do better myself. 'Course I'd have had to write it out," she added modestly.

"Caesar was smart enough to wait for his fleet of warships when he saw he wasn't winning," said Abijah thoughtfully. "I'd guess there's a lesson there—don't run ahead of your ability and your help! And you've been my fleet for nearly four years, now, helping me when I'd have lost the battle alone."

"You can certainly thank the Lord and Squire Bean," Rebecca reminded Abijah.

"And that reminds me," he answered thoughtfully, "The squire's taking me over to Bowdoin College in Brunswick next week for an interview with the dean. Squire says if I can impress 'em with Latin and do well on the entrance exams, I may get in on probation. If I pass the first year, I'll be a reg'lar student then, on my way to a degree."

"Oh, 'Bijah!" Rebecca dropped the Latin book into the pile of bean vines. "I thought you'd be lucky to get into Wareham Academy! But college! Can you imagine it? Why, all along I've encouraged you to *think* of college—but I meant . . . I guess I meant after high school."

"Hey, I'm almost twenty," Abijah interjected. "Who wants a nineteen-year-old freshman at the academy?"

Rebecca's reward in being Abijah's tutor lay primarily in the joy of watching this once-illiterate young man, nearly five years older than she, develop his mental capacity. And grow Abijah did! From practicing his consonants and vowel sounds in phonetic drills one week, Abijah, though his education had been postponed until after his sixteenth birthday, went to reading sentences the next. A week later he was reading whole pages—and reciting back to Rebecca a summary of each page as he went along. Such is the power of motivation harnessed to a sharp mind.

Within a month, Abijah graduated from the *Primer* to *McGuffey's First Reader*. That kept his attention for two weeks. The *Second Reader* required two more. The *Third, Fourth,* and *Fifth* each required a month to read; and the writing exercises that accompanied the literary selections in his books he laboriously wrote out in his almost illegible hand to be corrected and criticized by Squire Bean himself. The *Sixth Reader* occupied Abijah for four months, for he frequently digressed into reading the other works by the same authors to be found in the squire's well-stocked library. History, Abijah did not study — he devoured it, whole volumes at an evening's sitting.

For Rebecca's reward, also, there was the use of the squire's library, with its "complete works" sets of Dickens and Shakespeare, Gibbon's *Decline and Fall,* and Mather's *Magnalia Christi Americana.* Squire Bean had been a lawyer until he retired at fifty to become a gentleman farmer. He was fifty-three when Abijah Flagg joined his household, and his stock was considerably richer in books than in farming implements or cattle. On the Saco River, only the Reverend Baxter possessed a larger library.

The squire had never studied the gentle art of farming and relied on the memories of a youth left nearly four decades earlier, as well as the advice of his less-lettered but more-experienced neighbors. True, he had always been a tolerably good gardener, and this sustained him through seasons when his sheep jumped the fence, his cows did not calve in season, and his chickens would not hatch their eggs.

Abijah Flagg's romance with Emma Jane Perkins had been going on, so far as Abijah was concerned, for many years. His affection dated back to his thirteenth year when, at age nine, Emma Jane had accompanied her father one late spring day to the Bean farm to check on his welfare and to ascertain how he and the squire were getting on. Emma Jane had shown no sign of reciprocating his attachment until recent years, when the evolution of the chore boy into the budding scholar and man of affairs had enflamed her interest in him. Rebecca had been Abijah's tutor since she was twelve, and her reports of his phenomenal progress kept Emma Jane in awe.

Squire Bean and his wife had taken Abijah away from the town poor farm, thinking that they could make him of some little use about the house and around the squire's farm. Abbie Flagg, Abijah's mother, had been neither wise nor beautiful. It is to be feared that she was not even good, and her lack of all these desirable qualities, particularly the last one, had been impressed upon the boy by scornful — and sometimes jealous — neighborhood rascals ever since he could remember.

People seemed to blame Abijah for being in the world at all — this world that had not expected him nor desired him nor made any provision for him. The great battle-ax of opinion was forever leveled at his merest transgression, no matter how innocent, though it must be confessed that Abijah had on occasion gone out of his way to live up to his reputation as a transgressor. He had grown sad, shy, clumsy, stiff, and self-conscious. He had an indomitable craving for love in his heart, but he had seldom received a caress in his life.

Abijah became more contented when he came to Squire Bean's house, since usefulness adds satisfaction to the life of the individual, be he child or adult. The first year there he not only cut the seed potatoes, but he was assigned to pick up chips, carry pine wood into the kitchen, go to the post office, run errands, drive the cows to pasture, and feed the hens. Every day he grew more and more useful, and by fall he could guide the plow like a man as the squire's plodding, heavy-hooved gray Percherons turned the rocky hillside soil into furrows. By the time he was fifteen, Abijah's prowess with an ax and a scythe were matters of legend across the Saco Valley.

One never-to-be-forgotten day early in his stay at Squire Bean's, Abijah was returning from the post office in Riverboro Village with the squire's mail. He had just crossed the bridge from the village, and passing Perkins's blacksmithy he was about to ascend the mile-long hill which led to Squire Bean's farm. But he spied Emma Jane, a pretty, chubby doll of a nine-year-old girl she was, with bright fuzzy hair, pink cheeks, china-blue eyes, and a smile of almost bewildering continuity. He returned her smile with a smile of his own—an expression seldom seen on his sad face. "Hi, 'Bijah," Emma Jane shyly greeted him.

Abijah had seen Emma Jane before, of course. But she suddenly moved from the shadows of his mind into the bright light of day with that greeting. It is not the form of woman but her siren voice that most enthralls the masculine passion. And immature though his yearnings were, they were awakened by Emma Jane's friendly greeting. Though she had no interest in him, it was enough. Suddenly he became a person of worth—worth enough to imagine that another might want to speak to him.

"Hi, yourself!" At that point Mrs. Perkins appeared, marched Emma Jane inside, and slammed the door.

Then came the Fourth of July holiday, when Jimmy Watson, whose acquaintance Abijah had made on his forays to Watson's Mercantile for Mrs. Bean, came over to play. Jimmy appeared halfway between Bean's farm and the Perkins's residence with Emma Jane in tow. Abijah, taking his cue from Mrs. Perkins's lesson in selective companionship, curtly ordered little Jimmy home, then proceeded to walk with Emma Jane behind a pasture stone wall where he might entertain her on his own terms. Within moments, Emma Jane and Abijah were playing house in a makeshift cabin of old cedar rails leaning against the wall. Mrs. Perkins, thinking her daughter safely in the company of the respectable son of the merchant for the time being, was none the wiser.

Jimmy, after considering the matter for some moments, decided to rejoin the pair who had so rudely thrust him out. At that moment Abijah, who though indeed curt, had until then been relatively sanguine, was seized with fury, and he threw stones until Jimmy ran crying back to the village. Then he made a door of sticks to the playhouse, pushed the awed Emma Jane inside, and strode up and down in front of the crude edifice like an Indian brave. At such an early age does woman become a distracting and disturbing influence in man's career!

Time went on, and so did the rivalry between the poor-house boy and the son of the merchant. But Abijah's chances of friendship with Emma Jane grew fewer and fewer as they both grew older. Abijah did not go to school, so there was no meeting ground there, save for occasional excursions at recess time. He did attend church with Squire and Mrs. Bean at the Tory Hill Meeting House, but the fleeting glimpses he gained of Emma Jane across the crowded meetinghouse could only serve to whet his appetite for her companionship.

Sometimes the squire would in good humor let Abijah leg it over to the schoolhouse in time for the noon recess, and Abijah joined the knot of older boys and girls at play at the back of the school lot near the woods. As his rival Jimmy Watson was particularly small and fragile, Abijah generally chose feats of strength and skill for these noon-time performances, always designed to impress Emma

Jane. Sometimes he would throw his straw hat up into the lonesome pine as far as he could, and when it came down, catch it on his head. Sometimes he would walk on his hands with his legs wriggling in the air or turn a double somersault or jump incredible distances across the extended arms of the Simpson twins. His chest swelled with pride when the girls exclaimed, "Isn't he splendid!" although he had often heard his rival scornfully murmur, "Smart aleck!" Always, though, when the school bell rang, Abijah's audience left, and he was obliged to shuffle back to the farm for several more hours of chores.

Squire Bean, although he did not send the boy to school thinking at first that since he was of no possible importance in the universe, it was not worth bothering about his education and—having been appraised of the circumstances of Abijah's expulsion from school—finally became impressed with his ability. So he lent him books and gave him more time to study. These were all he needed—books and time and motivation. And when there was an especially hard knot to untie, Rebecca, as the star scholar of the neighborhood, helped him untie it.

From the time he was seventeen, Abijah longed to go away from Riverboro and be something better than a chore boy. Squire Bean had been giving him small wages for three or four years which he had carefully saved in an old tobacco tin tucked under the eaves of the farmhouse shed. Too, Abijah learned of a scholarship for orphans set up at Bowdoin College. Since he had never been formally adopted by the Beans, he felt certain he would qualify. The great hurdle, of course, was the college entrance exams, and passing these was a dream Abijah seldom dared allow himself.

When at age twenty the time of parting came, the squire presented Abijah with a double eagle—a twenty dollar gold piece—and a silver-case Waltham pocket watch. "Every college man needs a good timepiece to help him keep track of his schedule," the squire had remarked magnanimously.

Many a time Abijah had discussed his future with Rebecca and asked her opinion. This was not strange, for there was nothing in human form that she could not and did not converse with, easily and delightedly. And her own "half-orphaned" girlhood had made her a sympathetic listener as he freely poured out his ambitions.

Rebecca had ideas on every conceivable subject, and she would cheerfully have advised the minister if he had asked her. The fishman consulted her when he couldn't endure his mother-in-law another minute in the house. Uncle Jerry Cobb didn't sell his river field until he had talked it over with Rebecca. And as for Aunt Jane, she couldn't decide whether to wear her black merino coat or her gray mohair unless Rebecca cast the final vote.

Abijah wanted to go far away from Riverboro, as far as Bowdoin College in Brunswick, which was at least forty miles. Although this seemed extreme, Rebecca agreed, saying pensively, "There *is* a kind of magicness about going far away and then coming back all changed."

"Far away," to Rebecca, had once meant to leave dear Sunnybrook to dwell with her aunts in the brick house in Riverboro. But Riverboro was now her home. Her faraway places had become the cities of her books—London, Paris, Rome, Jerusalem.

This was precisely Abijah's unspoken thought. Bowdoin knew nothing of the awful stigma of his poor-house roots so that he could start fair. He would have gone to Wareham Academy and thus remained within daily sight of the beloved Emma Jane, and Rebecca had gently suggested this. But no, he was not going to permit her to watch him in the process of "becoming," but after he had "become something," she could inspect the finished product. Then, he felt, he could present his case to her affections.

Abijah did not propose to take any risks after all these years of silence and patience. He proposed to disappear, like the moon on a dark night. As he was at present something that Mr. Perkins would by no means have in the family, nor Mrs. Perkins allow in the house, he would neither return to Riverboro nor ask any favors of them until he had something to offer.

Yes sir, Abijah was going to be crammed to the eyebrows with learning—useless kinds and all. He was going to have good clothes and a good income. Everything that was in his power should be right, because there would always be lurking in the background the things he never could help—the unmarried mother, the drunken father, and the poor farm.

So Abijah went away, and although at Squire Bean's invitation he came back yearly for brief summer visits, and at Christmas and Easter, he was little seen in Riverboro. His visits in Riverboro were tantalizing rather than pleasant. Abijah was invited to a Christmas party during his first vacation from college, but he was all the time conscious of his shirt collar, and he was sure that his pants were not the proper thing, for his brief exposure to college life had caused his ideals of dress and manners to attain almost unreasonable heights.

They played "drop the handkerchief" at the party, but Abijah had not the audacity to kiss Emma Jane's cheek, which was bad enough, but Jimmy Watson had and did, which was infinitely worse! The sight of James Watson's unworthy and overly ambitious lips on Emma Jane's pink cheek almost destroyed his faith in God's ability to work

out his future. And that Emma Jane, though she blushed
with proper modesty, did not at once slap the impudent
Jimmy's brash face caused him to question whether his
faith in womanhood had been misplaced. Only Abijah's
recently acquired definition of a *gentleman* prevented him
from immediately expelling Watson from the party.

After the party was over, Abijah went back to his old
room in Squire Bean's shed chamber. As he lay in bed, his
thoughts fluttered about Emma Jane as swallows in summer circle around the eaves of the squire's old barn. The
terrible sickness of hopeless, handicapped love kept him
awake. Once he crawled out of bed in the night, lighted
the lamp, put a few drops of oil on his hair, and brushed it
violently for several minutes before his cracked and sil-
vered old mirror. Then he went back to bed. After making
up his mind that he would buy a banjo and learn to play it
so that he would be more attractive at parties and outshine
his rival in society as he had in athletics, he finally sank
into a troubled slumber.

12

THE CIRCLE OF GOLD

Thanksgiving weekend during Rebecca's second year at Wareham gave her opportunity to renew her old friendship with Clara Belle Simpson, a friendship which had been interrupted by Rebecca's sojourn at boarding school. It will be remembered that Clara Belle's parents, with their brood of children, had been expelled without ceremony from Riverboro and returned to Acreville, her father's habit of helping himself to others' property having reduced the Simpsons to pauperhood, while he found himself a frequent guest of the York County Jail.

Clara Belle, however, being an industrious though simple-minded girl, had been invited back to Riverboro by the Fogg family as a live-in baby sitter and chore girl. At fifteen, it was deemed that she had had quite enough education to suit her for life, and she now should be expected to learn household economics until a suitable husband should court her.

Clara Belle's chief responsibility in her employment was the Fogg infant, more popularly known as "the Fogg Horn," because of his lusty bawl, a cry which rivaled Hillard Robinson's hound as a source of irritation to the neighbors on quiet summer nights. As the child became a toddler, his bawl had become an interminable, piercing scream, which to the distress of the entire village he exercised whenever left alone for more than a few moments.

It was Saturday afternoon, and Rebecca's homework for Monday had been completed—the previous day, in fact. She took her coat from the hall closet, then paused at Aunt Miranda's rocker. "Bye, Aunty. I'm headin' out to Foggs to see Clara Belle. Be back in time for supper."

Though Rebecca was by now quite a young lady and generally used to coming and going as she pleased, Aunt Miranda was still reluctant to accept her niece's maturity. Miranda laid down her knitting and raised her eyes. "You know well enough, Rebecca, that I don't like you to be close friends with Abner Simpson's younguns," she said with a sigh. "They ain't fit company for anyone that's got Sawyer blood in their veins, if it's ever so little. I don't know, I'm sure, how you're goin' to turn out! And it's Abijah Flagg that you're everlastingly talkin' to lately. I should think you'd rather read some improvin' book than to be chatterin' with Squire Bean's chore boy!"

"He isn't always going to be a chore boy," explained Rebecca quietly, "and that's what we're considering. You know very well that he can't go to school, not having any parents, and I've been helping him with his studies since I was in the sixth grade—and now you bring it up! He can read now as well as anybody, and he wants to go to high school, and perhaps Bowdoin College when he can pass the entrance exams, if the minister's wife and I can continue to tutor him—though he seems to need us very little.

"And Clara Belle kind of belongs to the village, now that she lives with Mrs. Fogg. She was always the best behaved of all the girls, either in school or Sunday school. Children can't help who their fathers are!"

"Everybody says Abner Simpson is turnin' over a new leaf, and if so, his family ought to be encouraged every possible way," said Miss Jane, entering the room with her mending basket in hand.

"If Abner Simpson is turnin' over a new leaf or anything else in creation, it's only to see what's on the underside!" remarked Miss Miranda promptly. "Don't talk to me about new leaves! You can't change that kind of a man. He is what he is, and you can't make him no different!"

"The grace of God can do consid'rable," objected Jane mildly.

"I ain't sayin', but it can if it sets out, but it has to begin early and stay late on a man like Simpson."

"Now, Miranda, Abner ain't more'n forty! I don't know what the average age for repentance is in menfolks, but when you think of what an awful sight of 'em leaves it to their deathbeds, forty seems real kind of young. Not that I've heard Abner has become a Christian, but everybody's surprised at the good way he's conductin' himself this fall."

"They'll be surprised the other way 'round when they come to miss their firewood and apples and potatoes again," affirmed Miranda.

"Clara Belle don't seem to have inherited stealin' habits from her father," Jane ventured again timidly. "No wonder Mrs. Fogg sets such store by the girl. If it hadn't been for her, the baby would have been dead by now."

"Perhaps tryin' to save it was interferin' with the Lord's will," was Miranda's retort.

"Folks can't stop to figure out just what's the Lord's will when a child has upset a kettle of scalding water onto himself," and as she spoke Jane darned socks more excitedly. "Mrs. Fogg knows well enough she hadn't ought to have left that baby alone in the kitchen with the stove, even if she did see Clara Belle comin' up the road. She'd ought to have waited for her before drivin' off. But of course she was afraid of missing the train, and she's too good a woman to be held accountable."

"The minister's wife says Clara Belle is a female hero—a heroine's what Mrs. Baxter called her!" interrupted Rebecca.

"Clara Belle is the female of Simpson, that's what she is," Miss Miranda asserted. "But she's been brought up to use her wits, and I ain't sayin' but what she used them well for once."

"I should say she did," exclaimed Miss Jane. "To put that screamin', sufferin' child in the baby carriage and run all the way to the doctor's when there wasn't a soul on hand to advise her! Two or three more such actions would make the Simpson name sound consid'rable sweeter in this neighborhood."

"Simpson will always sound like Simpson to me!" darkly declared the elder sister. "But we've talked enough about 'em an' to spare. Go along, Rebecca. But remember that a girl is known by the company she keeps."

"All right, Aunt Miranda. Thank you," Rebecca answered, opening the door even as she uttered the words. She had had quite enough of Aunt Miranda's self-righteous rantings for one day.

There was a sharp frost in the air, but a bright, cheery sun shown as Rebecca hurried out of the brick house yard. Emma Jane Perkins was away over Sunday on a visit to a cousin in North Riverboro. Alice Robinson and Candace Milliken were in bed with the flu, and Riverboro was very quiet. Still, life was seldom anything but a happy adventure to Rebecca, and she started afresh every morning to its conquest. The mile walk to call on freckled, red-haired Clara Belle Simpson, whose face Miss Miranda said looked like a raw pie in a brick oven—these commonplace incidents were sufficiently exhilarating to brighten her eye and quicken her step.

As the great bare horse chestnut tree near the gate of the Fogg residence loomed into view, Rebecca could see a slight, red-haired girl in a gray coat running down the long path to meet her. The girls embraced each other ardently.

"I'm so glad you could come," exclaimed Clara Belle. "I was so afraid the fish peddler wouldn't tell you I wanted to see you, or your Aunt Miranda wouldn't let you come."

Rebecca laughed aloud at the last remark. "Aunt Miranda *is* taking my growing up rather hard," she said, "but she pretty much lets me decide my goings and comings. You're not homesick any more, are you?" she added.

"No-o, not really. Only when I remember Mother has to manage Susan and the twins—they get ornerier and ornerier the older they get, seems like. But they're really gettin' on well enough without me. But Rebecca, I kind of think I'm going to be given away to the Foggs for good."

"Do you mean adopted?"

"Yes. I think Father's going to sign papers. You see, we can't tell how many years it'll be before the poor Fogg baby outgrows its burns, and Mrs. Fogg'll never be the same again, and she must have somebody to help her."

"You'll be their real daughter then, won't you, Clara Belle? And Mr. Fogg is a church deacon and a town selectman and a road commissioner. Everybody in Riverboro thinks he's such a fine man!"

"Yes. I'll have board and clothes and an allowance and be named Fogg, and"—here her voice sank to an awed whisper—"the upper farm if I should get married. Miss Dearborn, our old teacher, told me that herself, when she was persuadin' me not to mind being adopted."

*The great bare horse chestnut tree near the gate
of the Fogg residence loomed into view.*

"Clara Belle Simpson-Fogg!" exclaimed Rebecca teasingly. "Who'd have thought you'd be a heroine and an heiress besides?"

"Of course, I know it's all right," Clara Belle replied soberly. "I'll have a good home, and Father can't keep us all. But it's kind of dreadful to be given away, like a piano or a horse and carriage!"

Rebecca's hand went out sympathetically to Clara Belle's freckled paw. Suddenly she whispered confidentially, "I'm not sure, Clara Belle, but what I'm given away, too. Poor Father left us in debt, you see. I thought I came away from Sunnybrook to get an education and then help pay off the mortgage. But Mother doesn't say anything about my coming back, and our family's one of those too-big ones, you know, just like yours." Clara Belle's worry melted into glad acceptance at Rebecca's empathy and identification with her in her plight.

"Did your mother sign adoption papers to your aunts?" Clara Belle inquired.

"If she did I never heard anything about it," Rebecca admitted.

"You'd know if 'twas a real adoption. I guess you're lent," Clara Belle said cheeringly. "I don't believe anybody'd ever give *you* away! And, oh, Rebecca, Father *is* getting on better! He's worked on Daly's farm for more'n a year, now. They raise lots of horses and cattle, too, and he breaks all the young colts and trains them and swaps off the poor ones and drives all over the county. Daly told Mr. Fogg that Father is splendid with stock, and Father says it's just like play. He usually sends home money on Saturday nights, and sometimes he comes home, too."

"I'm so glad!" exclaimed Rebecca sympathetically. "Now your mother's happier and has food enough to fix decent meals for the children, doesn't she?"

"I don't know," sighed Clara Belle, "for I don't get back much. She *tries* to put on a good meal when I do go home." Her voice grew grave. "Ever since I can remember she's just washed and cried and cried and washed. Miss Dearborn spends her vacation up to Acreville, you know, and she came back to Riverboro this fall to board next to us, over t' the brown house. I heard her talkin' with Mrs. Fogg last night when I was rockin' the baby to sleep—I couldn't help it, they were so close—and Miss Dearborn said Mother doesn't like Acreville, though it's been near two years. She says nobody takes any notice of her, and they don't give her much work. Mrs. Fogg said, well, they were dreadful stiff and particular up that way, and they liked women to have weddin' rings."

"Hasn't your mother got a wedding ring?" asked Rebecca evenly.

"Mother hasn't got any jewelry, not even a breast pin."

"Well," Rebecca's tone was somewhat censorious, "your father's been so poor perhaps he couldn't afford a breast pin, but I should have thought he'd have given your mother a wedding ring when they were married. That's the time to do it."

"They didn't have any real church dress-up weddin'," explained Clara Belle sadly. "You see the first mother, mine, had the big boys and me, and then she died when we were little. Then after a while this mother came along to housekeep, and she stayed. And by and by Father and she went before Judge Hingham, and she became Mrs. Simpson. Susan and the twins and the baby are hers. But she and Father didn't have time or money for a reg'lar

weddin' in the church. They didn't have veils and brides-
maids and refreshments like Miss Dearborn's sister did."

"Do they cost a great deal — wedding rings?" asked Rebecca thoughtfully. "They're solid gold, so I s'pose they
do," she added. "If they were cheap enough, we might buy
one. I've got three or four dollars saved up. How much do
you have?"

"Less than a dollar," grieved Clara Belle. "And anyway there are no jewelry stores nearer than Milltown.
We'd have to buy it secretly, for I wouldn't want to make
Father angry or shame his pride, now he's got steady
work. I think maybe Mrs. Fogg'll let me have an advance
on my allowance if I explain things," Clara Belle said
hopefully.

Rebecca looked confounded. "I declare," she said, "I
think the Acreville people must be perfectly horrid not to
call on your mother only because she hasn't got a ring.
Wedding rings are special, for sure, but they are married,
so folks shouldn't shame 'em. You wouldn't dare tell your
father what Miss Dearborn heard so he'd save up and buy
the ring?"

"No, I certainly would not!" and Clara Belle's lips
closed tightly and decisively.

"I think we could get it from Mr. Aladdin, and I
needn't tell him who it's for," Rebecca said hesitatingly.
"But I'd feel foolish asking him. Still . . ."

"Then we'll have to forget it. Forgive me for mention-
ing it," said Clara Belle.

"No, no," objected Rebecca. "Mr. Aladdin's in North
Riverboro with his aunt for the Thanksgiving holiday. I'll
ask him to buy a ring for us in Boston. I won't explain
anything, you know. I'll just say I need a wedding ring,"
she concluded decisively. Secretly, however, Rebecca
wondered not only how she could get the message to Mr.

Aladdin, but how she could possibly explain things to him if she were to talk with him. Her sympathy for the Simpsons fought with a powerful urge to forget the whole matter.

"That would be perfectly lovely," replied Clara Belle, a look of hope dawning in her eyes. "And we can think afterward how to get it over to Mother. Perhaps you could send it to Father instead, but I wouldn't dare to do it myself. You won't tell anybody, Rebecca?"

"You know I wouldn't repeat a secret like that! With your permission, I shall tell Mr. Aladdin what's necessary, however. Can we meet next Saturday afternoon, and I'll tell you then what's happened? Why, Clara Belle, isn't that Mr. Aladdin watering his horse at the foot of the hill this very minute? It is! He's all alone, and I can ride home with him and ask him about the ring right away!"

Clara Belle kissed Rebecca's cheek fervently and turned up the path to Foggs, while Rebecca waited quietly at the top of the long hill, as Mr. Aladdin turned his horse up the street and trotted straight in her direction. Adam Ladd — Mr. Aladdin to Rebecca — drew up quickly when he spied Rebecca standing by Fogg's gate, her feminine modesty repressing the urge to flag him down. "Well, well, here is Rebecca Rowena perched beside the high road like a red-winged blackbird! Are you going to fly home or drive with me?"

Rebecca clambered into the carriage, laughing and blushing with delight at his nonsense and with joy at seeing him again. "Clara Belle and I were talking about you this very minute, and I'm so glad you came this way. There's something rather . . . very . . . important to ask you about," she began coyly.

"No doubt," laughed Adam, who had become in the course of his acquaintance with Rebecca a sort of high court of appeals. "I hope the premium banquet lamp doesn't smoke as it grows older?"

"Now, Mr. Aladdin, you *will* not remember nicely. Mr. Simpson swapped off the banquet lamp when he was moving the family to Acreville. It's not the lamp at all. But once, when I saw you last, you said you'd made up your mind what you were going to give me for Christmas."

"I do remember that much quite nicely."

"Well, is it bought?" she earnestly inquired.

"No, I never buy my Christmas presents before Thanksgiving."

"Then *dear* Mr. Aladdin, would you buy me something different, something that I want to give away, and buy it a little sooner than Christmas?"

"That depends. I don't relish having my Christmas presents given away. I like to have them kept forever in pretty girls' bureau drawers, all wrapped in pink tissue paper. But explain the matter and perhaps I'll change my mind. What is it you want?"

"I need a wedding ring," Rebecca said quietly, "and it's a special secret."

Adam's eyes flashed with surprise, and he smiled to himself with pleasure. Had he on his list of acquaintances, he asked himself, any person so altogether irresistible and unique as this delightful young lady? Then he turned to face her with the merry, teasing look that made him so delightful to young people.

"I thought it was perfectly understood between us," he said, "that if you could ever contrive to grow up and I were willing to wait, that I was to ride up to the brick house on my snow white . . ."

"Coal black," corrected Rebecca with a sparkling eye and a warning finger.

"Coal black charger, put a golden circlet on your lily white finger, draw you up behind me on my saddle . . ."

"And Emma Jane Perkins, too," Rebecca interrupted, playing his game.

"I think I didn't mention Emma Jane," argued Mr. Aladdin amicably. "Three on a saddle is very uncomfortable. I think Emma Jane leaps on the back of a prancing chestnut, and we all go off to my castle in the forest."

"Emma Jane never leaps, and she'd be afraid of a prancing chestnut," objected Rebecca.

"Then she shall have a gentle, cream-colored pony. But now, without any explanation, you ask me to buy a wedding ring, which shows plainly that you are planning to ride off on a snow white — I mean coal black — charger with somebody else."

Rebecca dimpled and laughed at Adam's nonsense. In her well-ordered world, no one but Adam Ladd played the game and answered the fool according to his folly. Nobody else talked delicious fairy story twaddle like Mr. Aladdin. "The ring isn't for *me!*" she explained carefully, forgetting in her embarrassment that he, of course, knew that very well. "The ring is for a friend."

"Why doesn't the groom give it to his bride himself?"

"Because he's poor and kind of thoughtless, and anyway she isn't a bride anymore. She has three step and three regular children."

Adam Ladd put his horsewhip back in its socket thoughtfully, and then he stooped to tuck in the rug over Rebecca's feet and his own. When he raised his head again he asked, "Why not tell me a little more, Rebecca? I'm safe."

Rebecca looked at him, feeling his wisdom and strength and above all, his sympathy. Then she said hesitatingly, "You remember I told you all about the Simpsons that day on your aunt's porch when you bought the soap because I told you how much they needed a banquet lamp? Mr. Simpson, Clara Belle's father, has always been very poor, and not always very good — a little bit thievish, you know — but oh, so pleasant and nice to talk to! And now they say he's turning over a new leaf. He's got a job, but they still don't have much money, because the folks in Acreville won't give Mrs. Simpson washings and ironings like they did in Riverboro.

"Everybody in Riverboro liked Mrs. Simpson when she came here as a stranger," Rebecca continued. "They were sorry for her, and she was so patient and such a hard worker and so kind to the children. The neighbors all knew then that they were married at the York County Courthouse by Judge Hingham, and that made a difference."

"That could certainly make a difference," Adam agreed.

"But where the Simpsons live now, though they used to know Mrs. Simpson when she was a girl, they gossip about her. Clara Belle heard Miss Dearborn say to Mrs. Fogg that the Acreville people are stiff and despise her because she doesn't wear a wedding ring like all the rest. They . . . they think the Simpsons are living in sin!" Rebecca concluded.

"She's got a problem, that's for sure," Adam murmured.

"Clara Belle and I thought that since they are so mean we'd love to give her a ring. Then she'd be happier and perhaps have more work. Perhaps if Mr. Simpson gets along better, Clara says, he will buy her a breast pin and earrings, and she'll be fitted out like the others," Rebecca remarked. As she had gotten into her explanation of the plight of Mrs. Simpson, Rebecca's initial embarrassment at asking for the ring had quite vanished. Such is the result of thinking of the needs of others.

Adam turned again to meet the luminous, innocent eyes that glowed under the delicate brows and long lashes, feeling as he had more than once felt before, as if his worldly wise thoughts had been bathed in some purifying spring. "How shall you send the ring to Mrs. Simpson?" he asked with interest.

"We haven't settled that yet. Clara Belle's afraid to do it, and she thinks I could manage better. Will the ring cost much?"

"It costs the merest trifle. I'll buy one and bring it to you at Wareham Academy, and we'll consult about it then. Somehow I can't picture myself rendering an adequate explanation to your Aunt Miranda if I brought it to the brick house," he chuckled. "I think as you're great friends with Mr. Simpson you'd better send it to him in a letter, letters being your strong point! It's a present a man ought to give his own wife, but it's worth trying, Rebecca. You and Clara Belle can manage it between you when you come back to Riverboro on a weekend. I'll stay in the background where nobody will see me."

13

ABNER SIMPSON'S NEW LEAF

M eantime, in these frosty autumn days, life was crowded with events in the lonely Simpson house at Acreville. The tumbledown dwelling stood on the edge of Pliny's Pond, so called because old Colonel Richardson had left his lands to be divided in five equal parts, each share to be chosen in turn by one of his five sons—Pliny, the eldest, having priority of choice.

Pliny Richardson, having little taste for farming and being ardently fond of fishing, rowing, and swimming, acted up to his reputation of being "a little mite odd," and he took most of his inheritance in water—hence Pliny's Pond.

On the shore of that small lake Pliny Richardson had erected a house—more properly a cabin, nicely shingled with cedar and sturdily framed, but barren of plaster and ceilings within. And having no foundation save the stones laid on bare earth to support its sills, the dwelling twisted and turned with the seasons until the frame was quite out of plumb. Pliny himself had grown old and died, and having no heirs, his cabin had become the property of the town of Acreville, which let it out without rent to a series of impoverished families needing a roof. A roof was about all that was left of the house on Pliny's Pond when the Simpson's moved in with their furnishings, such as they were.

Since his family had come to Acreville, the eldest Simpson boy had left home and for some months had been working on a farm in Cumberland County. The middle one, Samuel, better known as "See-saw," had lately found a humble job laboring in a shingle mill and had become partially self-supporting.

Clara Belle had been adopted by the Foggs in Riverboro. Thus there were only three mouths to fill—the capacious ones of the rapidly growing twins, Elijah and Elisha, and of lisping little Susan, who had become a capable houseworker and mother's assistant. The Simpson baby had died a year earlier. Some thought it died of discouragement at having been born into a family unprovided with sufficient food or money or care, or even with desire for, or appreciation of, babies.

There was no doubt that the erratic father of the house had turned over a new leaf. Exactly when he began or how or why or how long he would continue the praiseworthy process—in a word whether there would be more leaves turned as the months went on—Mrs. Simpson did not know, and it is doubtful if any authority lower than that of Mr. Simpson's Maker could have decided the matter. He had stolen articles for swapping purposes for a long time, but had often avoided detection and had usually escaped punishment until the last few years.

Three fines imposed for small offenses were followed by several arrests and two imprisonments for brief periods by Judge Hingham, and Simpson thus found himself wholly out of sympathy with the wages of sin. Sin itself he did not especially mind, but its wages were becoming unpleasant and irksome to a family man with a wife and children. He also minded very much the isolated position in the community which over the years had become his, for Abner Simpson was a social being. He would *almost* rather not steal from a neighbor than have him find it out and cease association. This feeling had been working in him and rendering him irritable and depressed when he took his daughter back to Riverboro at the time of the great flag-raising the summer before Rebecca began her studies at Wareham.

There are seasons of refreshment, as well as seasons of drought, in the spiritual as in the natural world, and in some way or other dews and rains of grace fell upon Abner Simpson's heart during that brief journey to Riverboro. Perhaps the giving away of a child that he could not support had made the rocky soil of his heart a little softer and readier for planting than usual. But the day he stole the new flag off Mrs. Peter Meserve's doorstep under the impression that the cotton-covered bundle contained freshly washed clothes, he unconsciously set certain forces in operation.

It will be remembered that Rebecca had seen an inch of red bunting peeping from the back of his wagon and had asked the pleasure of a drive with him. She was no soldier of the regiment, but she proposed to follow that flag. When she diplomatically requested the return of the sacred object which was to be the glory of the grand flag-raising ceremony the next day, he discovered his mistake and was furious with himself for having slipped into a disagreeable predicament. Later, when Abner unexpectedly faced a detachment of angry Riverboro women at the crossroads and met not only their wrath and scorn, but the reproachful disappointment in Rebecca's eyes, he felt degraded as never before.

The night he had spent at the Center Tavern did not help matters, nor did the jolly patriotic meeting of the two villages at the flag-raising the next morning, when he was forced to watch from a distance, fearful of being tarred and feathered and driven out of town. He would have enjoyed being at the head and front of the festive preparations, but he had cut himself off from all such friendly gatherings. He intended at any rate to sit in his wagon on the very outskirts of the assembled crowd and see some of the gaity, for heaven knows he had little enough—he who loved talk and song and story and laughter and excitement. The flag was raised, the crowd cheered, the girl to whom he had lied, the girl who was impersonating the State of Maine, was on the platform speaking her poem, and he could just distinguish some of the words she was saying:

> For it's your star, my star,
>   all the stars together,
> That make our country's flag so proud
> To float in the bright fall weather.

Then suddenly there was a clarion voice ringing the air, and he saw a tall man standing in the center of the stage and heard him crying, "Three cheers for the girl that saved the flag from the hands of the enemy!"

Simpson was sore and bitter enough already—lonely, isolated from honest community life. He had no hand to shake, no neighbor's meal to share, and this unexpected public arraignment smote him between the eyes. With resentment newly kindled, pride wounded, vanity bleeding, he flung a curse at the joyous throng and drove toward home—the home where he would find his ragged, hungry children and meet the timid eyes of a woman who had been the loyal partner of his poverty and years of disgrace.

It is probable that even then his (extremely light) hand was already on his new leaf. Good fortune seemed to be on his side, for some months later it flung into Simpson's lap an interesting and agreeable employment where meager money could be earned by doing the very thing his nature craved. There were feats of daring to be performed in the sight of admiring and applauding stable boys; the horses he loved were his companions; he was *obliged* to swap and trade, since Daly, his new employer, counted on him to get rid of all undesirable stock. Power and responsibility of a sort were given to him freely, for tough-minded Daly felt himself amply capable of managing any number of Simpsons. So there were numberless advantages within the man's grasp, and wages besides! They were little more than boys' wages, to be sure, for such is the plight of a man who has not had a steady job for most of his adult life. But he was getting paid, and the remuneration seemed to give him courage to face each day.

Abner positively felt no temptation to steal. His soul expanded with pride, and the admiration and astonishment with which he regarded his virtuous present was only equaled by the disgust with which he contemplated his own crooked past. It had not been so much a vicious past, in his own generous estimation of it, as a "thunderin' foolish" one.

Mrs. Simpson took the same view of Abner's new leaf as did her husband. She was thankful for his new season of honesty coupled with the Saturday evening pay envelope. Though the truth of the matter is that there were weekends when the pay envelope did not reach her hands; on others, the pittance left after Abner's tobacco and card money would scarce buy old potatoes enough for seven more days. If she still washed and cried and cried and washed, as Clara Belle had always seen her, it was either because of some hidden sorrow or because her poor strength seemed all at once to have deserted her.

14

THE GREEN ISLE

Just when employment and good fortune had come to the stepchildren and her own were better fed and clothed than ever before, the pain that had always lurked, constant but dull, near Mrs. Simpson's heart, grew fiercer and stronger. It clutched her in its talons, biting, gnawing, worrying, leaving her as the months wore on with weaker powers of resistance.

Still, hope was in the air, and a greater content than had been hers for years was in her eyes. It was a content that came near to happiness until the doctor ordered her to keep to her bed and sent for Clara Belle.

"Is your pain bad today, mother?" asked Clara Belle, who, only lately adopted, was merely borrowed back from Mrs. Fogg for what was thought to be a brief emergency.

"Well, there, I can't hardly tell, Clara Belle," Mrs. Simpson replied, with a faint smile. "I can't seem to remember the pain these days without it's extra bad. The neighbors have become so kind — Mrs. Little has sent me canned mustard greens, and Mrs. Benson has sent mince pie. There's the doctor's morphine drops to make me sleep, and these blankets and that great box of groceries from Mr. Ladd. And you here to keep me comp'ny! I declare, I'm kind o' dazed with comforts."

Mr. Simpson had come briefly to see his wife and had met the doctor just as he was leaving the house. "She looks awful bad to me. Is she goin' to pull through all right, same as the last time?" he asked the doctor nervously.

"She's going to pull right through into the other world," the doctor answered bluntly. "And as there don't seem to be anybody else to take the bull by the horns, I'd advise you, having made the woman's life about as hard and miserable as you could, to try and help her to die easy!"

Abner, surprised and crushed by the weight of this verbal chastisement, sat down on the doorstep, his head in his hands, and thought a while solemnly. Serious thinking was not an operation he was used to indulging in, and when he opened the gate a few minutes later and walked slowly toward the lean-to shelter for his horse, he looked pale and unnerved. It is uncommonly startling first to see yourself in another man's scornful eyes, and then clearly in your own.

Two days later Simpson came home again, and this time he found Parson Baxter tying his piebald mare at the hitching post. Clara Belle's quick eye had observed the minister as he alighted from his buggy, and warning her mother, she hastily smoothed the bedclothes, arranged the medicine bottles, and swept the hearth.

"Oh, don't let him in!" wailed Mrs. Simpson, all of a flutter at the prospect of such a visitor. "Oh, dear! They must think over to Riverboro that I'm dreadful sick, or the minister wouldn't never think of callin'! Abner has druv every preacher away that's ever called at our house. Don't let him in, Clara Belle! I'm afraid he will say hard words to me, or pray for me, and I ain't never been prayed for since I was a child! Is Mrs. Baxter with him?"

"No, he's alone. But Father's just druv up and is hitching at the shed door."

"That's worse than all!" And Mrs. Simpson raised herself feebly on her pillows and clasped her hands in despair. "You mustn't let them two meet, Clara Belle, and you must send Reverend Baxter away. Your father wouldn't have a minister in the house nor speak to one for a million dollars!"

"Be quiet, Mother! Lie down! It'll be all right! You'll only fret yourself into a spell! The minister's just a good man. He won't say anything to frighten you. Father's talking with him real pleasant, and he's even pointing the way to the front door."

The parson knocked and was admitted by the excited Clara Belle who ushered him tremblingly into the sickroom. Then she took herself to the kitchen with the children as he gently requested her.

Abner Simpson, left alone in the shed, fumbled in his vest pocket and took out an envelope which held a sheet of paper and a tiny packet wrapped in tissue paper, both of which had lain in his pocket for some days. The letter had been read once before and ran as follows:

Dear Mr. Simpson:

This is a personal letter to you. I have heard that the Acreville people aren't nice to Mrs. Simpson because she doesn't have any wedding ring like all the others.

I know you've always been poor, dear Mr. Simpson, and troubled with a large family like ours at Sunnybrook Farm. But you really ought to have given Mrs. Simpson a ring when you were married to her, right at the very first. Then it would have been over and done with, as they are solid gold and last forever. And probably she wouldn't feel like asking you for one, because I know myself that I'd certainly be ashamed to beg for jewelry when just board and clothes cost so much. So I sent you a nice, new wedding ring to save your buying, thinking you might get Mrs. Simpson a bracelet or eardrops for Christmas. It did not cost me anything, as it was a secret present from a friend.

I hear Mrs. Simpson is sick, and it would be a great comfort to her while she is in bed and has so much time to look at it and enjoy it.

Please don't be angry with me, dear Mr. Simpson. I am so glad you are happy with the horses and colts. I believe now that you did think the flag was a bundle of washing when you took it that day, so no more from your

Trusted Friend,

Rebecca Randall

Simpson tore the rumpled letter slowly and quietly into fragments and scattered the bits on the woodpile. He took off his hat and smoothed his hair. He pulled his mustaches thoughtfully, straightened his shoulders, and then holding the tiny packet in the palm of his hand, he went 'round to the front door. Having entered the house, he stood outside the sickroom for an instant, turned the knob, and walked in softly.

Then, at last, the angels must have enjoyed a moment of unmixed joy, for in that brief walk from shed to house, Abner Simpson's conscience waked to life and attained sufficient strength to prick and sting, to provoke to remorse, to incite to penitence, to do all sorts of divine and beautiful things it was meant for but had never been allowed to do.

Clara Belle went about the kitchen quietly, making preparations for the children's supper. She had left Riverboro in haste, as the change for the worse in Mrs. Simpson had been very sudden. But since she had come she had thought more than once about the wedding ring. She had wondered whether Mr. Ladd had bought it for Rebecca and whether Rebecca would find means to send it to Acreville. But her cares had been so many and varied that the subject had now finally retired to the background of her mind.

The hands of the clock crept on, and Clara Belle hushed the strident, quarrelsome tones of Elijah and Elisha. She opened and shut the oven door to look at the corn bread. She advised Susan as to her dishes and marveled that the minister stayed so long.

At last she heard a door open and close and saw the parson come out, wiping his spectacles, and step into the buggy for his drive back to Riverboro. Then there was another period of suspense during which the house was as silent as a grave. Presently her father came into the kitchen, greeted the twins and Susan, and said to Clara Belle, "Don't go in there yet!" jerking his thumb toward their mother's room. "She's all beat out, and she's just dropping off to sleep. I'll send some groceries up from the store as I go back to my job. Is the doctor makin' a secunt call tonight?"

"Yes. He'll be here pretty soon now," Clara Belle answered, looking at the clock.

"All right. I'll be here again tomorrow, soon as it's light. If she ain't picked up any, I'll send word back to Mr. Daly that I gotta have some time off work, and I'll stop here with you for a spell till she's better."

It was true. Mrs. Simpson was "all beat out." It had been a time of excitement and stress, and the poor, fluttered creature was dropping off into the strangest sleep — a sleep made up of waking dreams. The pain that had encompassed her heart like a band of steel lessened its cruel pressure, and finally left her so completely that she seemed to see it floating above her head, only it looked no longer like a band of steel but a golden circle.

The frail bark in which she had sailed her life's voyage had been rocking on a rough and tossing ocean, and now it floated, floated slowly into smoother waters. As long as she could remember, her boat had been flung about in storm and tempest, lashed by angry winds, borne against rocks, beaten, torn, buffeted. Now the waves had subsided; the sky was clear; the sea was warm and tranquil; the sunshine dried the tattered sails; the air was soft and balmy.

And now, for sleep plays strange tricks, the bark disappeared from the dream, and it was she herself who was floating, floating farther and farther away, where, she neither knew nor cared. It was enough to be at rest, lulled by the lapping of the cool waves.

Then there appeared a green isle rising from the sea, an isle so radiant that her famished eyes could hardly believe its reality. But it *was* real, for she sailed nearer and nearer to its shore. At last her feet skimmed the shining sands, as she floated through the air as disembodied spirits float, till she sank softly at the foot of a spreading tree.

Then she saw that the green isle was a flowering isle, and from its very center gushed a river of water so crystalline, so clear, so sparkling that she felt that those waters must be life itself. She longed to drink until she could hold no more. Every shrub and bush of the isle was abloom and seemed to gather their source from the river. The trees were hung with rosy garlands, and even the earth was car-

peted with tiny flowers. The rare fragrances, the songs of
the birds, soft and musical, the ravishment of color, all
bore down upon her swimming senses at once, taking
them captive so completely that she remembered no past,
was conscious of no present, looked forward to no future.
She seemed to leave her worn-out body, and the sad,
heavy things of mortal existence fell behind. The humming
in her ears ceased; the circle of pain receded farther and
farther until it was lost to view.

Even the green isle now faded from her view, not into
darkness but into a light which seemed so to engulf it with
its dazzling that she could see nothing else. Instead she
saw a figure in white, a luminous, glowing splendor in
shepherd's clothing, yet with eyes of flame and hair and
beard as white as thistledown. And in His arms, cradled
ever so softly, rested the babe that had once so briefly
been hers. The man in white stretched forth a nail-scarred
hand. His lips parted. "Come," He uttered in tones of inef-
fable sweetness and majesty.

ta   ta   ta

It was time for the doctor now, and Clara Belle, too
anxious to wait any longer, softly turned the knob of her
mother's door and entered the room. The glow of the open
fire on the hearth illuminated the darkest side of the poor
chamber. There were no trees near the house, and a full
November moon streamed in at the uncurtained windows,
lighting up the interior—the unpainted floor, the bare, un-
plastered walls, and the white bedspread.

Her mother lay quite still, her head turned and droop-
ing a little on the pillow. Her left hand was folded softly
up against her breast, the fingers of the right partly covering it, as if protecting something precious. Was it the

moonlight that made the patient's brow so white, and where were the lines of anxiety and pain that had troubled her through the years? The face of the mother who had washed and cried and cried and washed was as radiant as if the closed eyes were beholding heavenly visions.

Something must have cured her! thought Clara Belle, awed and almost frightened by the whiteness and silence. Clara Belle struck a match to light the candle on the up-turned crate that served as a nightstand, that she might gain a better look at her sleeping mother. She was startled to find her grandmother's old Bible, which she knew had not been opened in years, left open beside the candle where Mr. Baxter, the minister, had laid it. Marked with a pencil was a verse which Clara Belle read with interest and awe:

> Jesus said unto her, I am the resurrection and the life: he that believeth in me, though he were dead, yet shall he live. (John 11:25)

Clara Belle bent to look more closely at the still, smiling shape and saw under the shadow of the caressing right hand a narrow gold band gleaming on the work-stained finger. "Oh, the ring came, after all!" she said in a glad whisper. "Perhaps it was what made her better!" She put her hand on her mother's gently. A terrified shiver, a warning shudder, shook the girl from head to foot at the chilling touch. A dread presence she had never met before suddenly took shape. It filled the room, stifled the cry on her lips, froze her steps to the floor, stopped the beat of her heart.

Just then the door opened.

"Oh, doctor! Come quick!" Clara Belle sobbed, stretching out her hand for help, then covering her eyes.

"Come close! Look at Mother! Is she better—or is she dead?"

He put one hand on the shoulder of the shrinking girl and touched the woman with the other.

"She is better," he said gently, "and she is dead."

15

AUNT MIRANDA'S DETERMINATION

The first happy year at Wareham, with its widened sky, its larger vision, its greater opportunity, was over and gone. Rebecca had studied during the summer vacation with the minister's wife as her tutor, and she had carried her load of household duties at the brick house, as well. On her return in the autumn, she had passed examinations which would enable her, if she carried out the same program the next season, to complete the course in three years instead of four.

Rebecca did wonderfully well in some of the required subjects and so brilliantly in others that the average score was respectable. She would never have been a remarkable scholar under any circumstances, perhaps, and she was easily outstripped in mathematics and the natural sciences by a dozen girls. But in some inexplicable way she became, as the months went on, the foremost figure in the school.

When Rebecca had entirely forgotten the facts which would enable her to answer a question fully and conclusively, she commonly had some original theory to expound. It was not always correct, but it was generally unique and sometimes amusing. She was only fair in Latin or French grammar, but when it came to translation, her freedom, her choice of words, and her sympathetic understanding of the spirit of the text made her the delight of her teachers and the despair of her rivals.

"She can be perfectly ignorant of a subject," said Miss Maxwell to Adam Ladd one day, "but entirely intelligent the moment she has a clue. Most of the other girls are full of information, but they are as unimaginative as sheep."

Rebecca's gifts had not been discovered except by the few during the first year when she was adjusting herself quietly to the situation. She was distinctly one of the poorer girls. She had no fine dresses to attract attention, no visitors, no friends in the town. She had more study hours and less time, therefore, for the companionship of other girls, gladly as she would have welcomed the gaiety of that side of school life.

Still, water will find its own level in some way, and by the spring of the second year, with the incident of the cannon behind her, she had naturally settled into the same sort of leadership which had been hers in the smaller community of Riverboro. She was elected assistant editor of the Wareham Academy *Pilot*, being the first girl to assume that enviable, though somewhat arduous and thankless position. When her first issue went to the Cobbs, Uncle Jerry and Aunt Sarah could hardly eat or sleep for pride.

"She'll always get votes," said Huldah Meserve, when discussing the election, "for whether she knows anything or not, she looks as if she did, and whether she's capable of filling an office or not, she looks as if she was. I only wish I was tall and dark and had the gift of making people believe I was great things, like Rebecca Randall. There's one thing, though — though the boys call her handsome, you notice they don't trouble her with much attention."

Rebecca's attitude toward the opposite sex was still somewhat indifferent and oblivious. No one could look at her and doubt that she had potentialities of feminine attraction latent within her somewhere, but that side of her nature was happily biding its time.

A human being is capable only of a certain amount of activity at a given moment and will inevitably satisfy first its most pressing needs, its most ardent desires, its chief ambitions. Rebecca was full of small anxieties and fears, for matters were not going well at the brick house. Too, she was so concerned over her mother's heavy mortgage on dear old Sunnybrook Farm that she often lost sleep at night. She was overbusy and overtaxed, and her thoughts were naturally drawn toward the difficult problems of daily living.

It had seemed to her during the autumn and winter of that year as if her Aunt Miranda Sawyer had never been, save at the very first, so censorious and so faultfinding. One Saturday Rebecca ran upstairs, and bursting into a flood of tears, exclaimed, "Aunt Jane, it seems as if I never could stand her continual scoldings. Nothing I can do suits Aunt Miranda. She's just said it will take me my whole life to get the Randall out of me, and I'm not convinced that I want it all out, so there we are!"

Aunt Jane, the younger of the "Sawyer girls," though seldom demonstrative, wept with Rebecca as she attempted to sooth her. "You must be patient," she said, wiping first her own eyes and then Rebecca's. "I haven't told you, for it isn't fair that you should be troubled when you're studying so hard, but your Aunt Miranda isn't well. One Monday morning about a month ago, she had a kind of fainting spell. It wasn't bad, but the doctor is afraid it was a stroke, and if so, it may be the beginning of the end. Seems to me she's been failing right along, and that's what makes her so fretful and easily vexed. She's had other troubles, too, that you don't know anything about. If you're not kind to your Aunt Miranda now, child, you'll be dreadful sorry sometime."

All the temper faded from Rebecca's face, and she stopped crying to say penitently, "Oh, the poor, dear thing! I won't mind a bit what she says now. She's just asked me for some milk toast, and I was dreading to take it to her. But this will make everything different. Don't worry yet, Aunt Jane, for perhaps it won't be as bad as you think."

So when she carried the toast to her aunt a little later, it was in the best gilt-edged china bowl, with a fringed napkin on the tray and a sprig of geranium lying across the saltcellar.

"Now, Aunt Miranda," she said cheerily, "I expect you to smack your lips and say this is good. It's not Randall, but Sawyer milk toast."

"You've tried all kinds on me, one time an' another," Miranda answered. "This tastes real kind o' good. But I wish you hadn't wasted that nice geranium."

"You can't tell what's wasted," said Rebecca philosophically. "Perhaps that geranium has been hoping this long time it could brighten somebody's supper, so don't disappoint it by making believe you don't like it. I've seen geraniums cry — in the very early morning!"

The mysterious trouble to which Jane had alluded was a very real one, but it was held in profound secrecy. Twenty-five hundred dollars of the Sawyer property had been invested in the business of a friend of their father's, and it had returned them a regular annual income of a hundred dollars. The family friend had been dead for some five years, but his son had inherited his interests and the business went on as formerly. Suddenly there came a letter saying that the firm had gone into bankruptcy, that the business had been completely lost, and that the Sawyer money had been swept away with everything else.

The loss of one hundred dollars a year is a very trifling matter to most folks, but it made all the difference between comfort and self-denial to the two old spinsters. Their manner of life had been so rigid and careful that it was difficult to economize any further. And the blow had fallen just when it was most inconvenient, for Rebecca's spring semester school tuition and boarding expenses, small as they were, had to be paid promptly and in cash.

"Can we possibly go on paying it? Shan't we have to give up and tell her why?" asked Jane tearfully of her elder sister.

"We have put our hand to the plow, and we can't turn back," answered Miranda in her grimmest tone. "We've taken her away from her mother and offered her an education, and we've got to keep our word. She's Aurelia's only hope for years to come, to my way o' thinkin'. Hannah's husband takes all her time 'n' thought, an' she's put her mother out o' sight and out o' mind. Rebecca's brother John, instead of farmin' like a sensible boy, thinks he must become a doctor—as if folks wasn't gettin' unhealthy enough these days, without turnin' out more young doctors to help 'em into their graves. No, Jane, we'll skimp 'n' do without, 'n' plan to git along on our interest money from our other investments somehow. But we won't break into our principal, whatever happens."

Breaking into the principal was in the minds of most thrifty New England women a sin second only to arson, theft, or murder. And, though the rule was occasionally carried too far for common sense, it doubtless wrought more of good than evil on the economy of the community.

Jane owned a nice stand of timber, it is true. But since the brick house was Miranda's—and she had changed her will a dozen times in as many years—fearful that she would be left bereft on her elder sister's death, Jane declined to sell off any lumber.

Rebecca, who knew nothing of their business affairs, merely saw her aunts grow more and more saving, pinching here and there, cutting off this and that relentlessly. Less meat and fish were bought. The woman who had lately been coming two days a week to do washing, ironing, and scrubbing was dismissed. The old bonnets of the season before were brushed up and retrimmed. There were no drives to Maplewood or trips to Portland. Economy was carried to its very extreme, but though Miranda was well-nigh as gloomy and uncompromising in her manner and conversation as a woman could be, she at least never accused her niece of being a burden. So Rebecca's share of the Sawyers' misfortunes consisted only in wearing her old dresses, hats, and jackets, without any apparent hope of a change.

There was, however, no concealing the state of things at Sunnybrook Farm, where chapters of accidents had unfolded themselves like a sort of serial story that had run through the year. The potato crop had failed, there were no apples to speak of, and the hay had been poor. Rebecca's mother, Aurelia, had dizzy spells, and Mark had broken his ankle. As this was his fourth accident, Miranda inquired how many bones there were in the human body, "so't they'd know when Mark got through breakin' 'em." The time for paying the interest on the mortgage, that incubus that had crushed all the joy out of the Randall household, had come and gone. And for the first time in fourteen years there was no possibility of paying the required forty-eight dollars.

The only bright spot on the horizon was Hannah's marriage to Will Melville, a young farmer whose land joined Sunnybrook. He had a good house, was alone in the world, and was his own master. Hannah was so satisfied with her own unexpectedly radiant prospects that she hardly realized her mother's anxieties.

Hannah had made a week-long visit at the brick house. Miranda's impression, conveyed in privacy to Jane, was that Hannah was "as tight as the bark on a tree and consid'able selfish, too, and that when she'd climbed as fur as she could in the world, she'd kick the ladder out from under her, everlastin' quick." On being sounded as to her ability to be of use to the younger children in the future, Hannah said "she guessed she'd done her share a'ready, and she wa'n't goin' to burden Will with her poor relations."

"She's like her grandmother, Susan Randall, through and through!" sputtered Miranda. "I was glad to see her face turned toward Temperance. If that mortgage is ever cleared from the farm, 'twon't be Hannah that'll do it. It'll be Rebecca or me!"

16

ALADDIN RUBS HIS LAMP

Y our esteemed contribution entitled 'Wareham Wildflowers' has been accepted for *The Pilot,* Miss Perkins," teased Rebecca with a flair, entering the dorm room where Emma Jane was darning her stockings. "I stayed to tea with Miss Maxwell, but I came home early to tell you."

"You are joking, Becky!" faltered Emma Jane, looking up from her work.

"Not a bit. The senior editor read it and thought it highly instructive. It will be printed in the next issue."

"Not in the same number with your poem about the golden gates that close behind us when we leave school?" And Emma Jane held her breath as she awaited the reply.

"Even so, Miss Perkins."

"Rebecca," said Emma Jane, with the nearest approach to tragedy that her nature would permit, "I don't know as I shall be able to bear it, and if anything happens to me, I ask you solemnly to bury that issue of *The Pilot* with me."

Rebecca did not seem to think this to be the expression of an exaggerated state of feeling for she replied, "I know.

That's just the way it seemed to me at first, and even now, whenever I'm alone and take out *The Pilot*'s back numbers to read over my contributions, I almost burst with pleasure. It's not that they are good, either, for they look worse to me every time I read them."

"If you would only live with me in some little house when we get older," mused Emma Jane, as with her darning needle poised in air she regarded the opposite wall dreamily, "I would do the housework and cooking and copy all your poems and stories and take them to the post office, and you needn't do anything but write. It would be perfectly elergant!"

"I'd like nothing better, if I hadn't promised to keep house for my brother, John," replied Rebecca.

"He won't have a house for a good many years, will he?"

"No," sighed Rebecca ruefully, flinging herself down at the table and resting her chin on her hand. "Not unless we can contrive to pay off that detestable mortgage. The day grows farther off instead of nearer, now that we haven't paid the interest this year."

She pulled a piece of paper towards her and scribbling idly on it read aloud in a moment or two:

"Will you pay a little faster?"
    said the mortgage to the farm;
"I confess I'm very tired of this place."
"The weariness is mutual,"
    Rebecca Randall cried;
"I wish I'd never gazed upon your face!"

"I didn't know that a mortgage had a face," observed Emma.

"Our mortgage has," said Rebecca revengefully. "I should know him if I met him in the dark. Wait, and I'll draw him for you. It will be good for you to know how he looks. Then when you have a husband and seven children, you won't allow him to come anywhere within a mile of your farm," she added, her tone between mirth and despair.

The sketch when completed was of a sort to be shunned by a timid person on the verge of slumber. There was a tiny house on the right, and a weeping family gathered in front of it. The mortgage was depicted as an ogre who held an axe uplifted in his right hand. A figure with streaming black locks was staying the blow, and this, Rebecca explained complacently, was intended as a likeness of herself, though she was rather vague as to the method she should use in thwarting the attack.

"He's terrible," said Emma Jane, "but awfully wizened and small."

"It's only a twelve-hundred-dollar mortgage," said Rebecca. "And that's called a small one. My brother, John, saw a man once that was mortgaged for twelve thousand."

"Will you become a writer or an editor when you graduate?" asked Emma Jane presently, as if one had only to choose and the thing were done.

"I shall have to do what turns up first, I suppose."

"Why not go out as a missionary to Africa, as the Burches are always coaxing you? The Board would pay your expenses."

"I can't make up my mind to be a missionary," Rebecca answered. "I would like to do something for somebody and make things move somewhere, but I don't want to go thousands of miles away to teach people how to live when I haven't learned myself."

❧ ❧ ❧

In these days Adam Ladd sometimes went to Temperance on business connected with a proposed new branch of the railroad of which he was a director. While there he gained an inkling of Sunnybrook affairs.

The building of the new road was not yet a certainty, and there was a difference of opinion as to the best route from Temperance to Lewiston. One route would lead directly through Sunnybrook from corner to corner, and Mrs. Randall would be paid handsomely for the farm. In the other route, her interests would not be affected, either for good or ill.

Coming from Temperance to Wareham one day, Adam had a long walk and talk with Rebecca, whom he thought looked pale and thin, though she was holding bravely to her self-imposed hours of work. She was wearing a black cashmere dress that had been her Aunt Jane's second best. Like Cinderella in the storybook, Rebecca's peculiar and individual charm seemed wholly independent of accessories. The lines of her figure and her rare coloring of skin and hair and eyes triumphed over shabby, second-hand clothing, though had the advantage of artistic apparel been given her, the little world of Wareham would probably at once have dubbed her a beauty. The long black braids were now disposed after a quaint fashion of her own. They were crossed behind, carried up to the front, and crossed again, the tapering ends finally brought down and hidden in the thicker part at the neck. Then a purely feminine touch was given to the hair that waved back from the face — a touch that rescued little crests and wavelets from bondage and set them free to take a new color in the sun.

Adam Ladd looked at her in a way that made her put her hands over her face and laugh through them shyly as she said, "I know what you are thinking, Mr. Aladdin — that my dress is an inch longer than last year and my hair different. But I'm not nearly a young lady yet—truly I'm not. Sixteen is a month off still, and you promised not to give me up till my dress trails on the floor. If you don't like me to grow old, why don't you grow young? Then we can meet in the halfway house and have nice times. Now that I think about it," she continued, "that's just what you've been doing all along. When you bought the soap, I thought you were Grandfather Sawyer's age; when you took me for that sleigh ride you seemed like my father. But when you showed me your mother's picture—and she in that photo no older than I—I felt as if you were Brother John, because I was so sorry for you."

"That will do very well," smiled Adam, "unless you grow old so swiftly that you become my grandmother before I really need one. You are studying too hard, Miss Rebecca Rowena!"

"Just a little," she confessed. "But vacation comes soon, you know."

"And are you going to have a good rest and try to recover your dimples? They are really worth preserving."

A shadow crept over Rebecca's face and her eyes fell. "Don't be kind, Mr. Aladdin, I can't bear it. It's . . . it's not one of my dimply days!" She ran in at the dormitory door and disappeared with a farewell wave of her hand.

Adam Ladd wended his way to the principal's office in a thoughtful mood. He had come to Wareham to unfold a plan that he had been considering for several days. This year was the fiftieth anniversary of the founding of the Wareham schools, and he meant to tell Mr. Morrison that in addition to his gift of a hundred volumes to the reference library, he intended to celebrate it by offering prizes in English composition, a subject in which he was much interested. He wished the boys and girls of the two upper classes to compete. The award would be made to the writ-

"And are you going to have a good rest and try to recover your dimples?"

ers of the two best essays. As to the nature of the prizes, he had not quite made up his mind, but they would be substantial ones, either of money or of books.

This interview accomplished, he called upon Miss Maxwell, thinking as he took the path through the woods to her apartment, "Rose Red-Snow White needs the help, and since there is no way of my giving it to her without causing gossip, she must earn it. I wonder if my money is always to be useless where most I wish to spend it!"

He had scarcely greeted his hostess when he said, "Miss Maxwell, doesn't it strike you that our friend Rebecca looks wretchedly tired?"

"She does indeed, and I am considering whether I can take her away with me. I always go to Nantucket Island for the spring vacation, traveling by boat to Old Point Comfort, and resting in our family's cottage. I should like nothing better than to have Rebecca for a companion."

"The very thing!" agreed Adam heartily. "But why should you take the whole responsibility? Why not let me help? I am greatly interested in the girl and have been for some years."

"You needn't pretend you discovered her," interrupted Miss Maxwell warmly, "for I did that myself."

"She was an intimate friend of mine long before she ever came to Wareham," laughed Adam, and he told Miss Maxwell the circumstances of his first meeting with Rebecca, of when she and Emma Jane had been peddling soap to help a needy family. "From the beginning I've tried to think of a way I could be useful in her development, but no reasonable solution seemed to offer itself."

"Luckily she attends to her own development," answered Miss Maxwell. "In a sense she is independent of everything and everybody. But she needs a hundred practical things that money would buy for her, and alas, I have a slender purse."

"Take mine, I beg, and let me act through you," pleaded Adam. "I could not bear to see even a young tree trying its best to grow without light or air — how much less a gifted child! I called on her aunts a year ago, hoping I might be permitted to give her a musical education. I assured them it was a most ordinary occurrence and that I was willing to be repaid later on if they insisted, but it was no use. The elder Miss Sawyer remarked that no member of her family had ever lived on charity, and she guessed they wouldn't begin at this late day."

"I rather like that uncompromising, small-town New England grit," Miss Maxwell said with a smile. "And so far I don't regret one burden that Rebecca has borne or one sorrow that she has shared. Necessity has only made her brave; poverty has only made her daring and self-reliant. As to her present needs," she continued firmly, "there are certain things only a woman ought to do for a girl, and I should not like to have you do them for Rebecca. I should feel that I was wounding her pride and self-respect, even though she were unaware of your aid. But there is no reason why *I* may not do them if necessary and let you pay her traveling expenses. I could accept those for her without the slightest embarrassment. But I agree that the matter would better be kept private between us."

"You are a real fairy godmother!" exclaimed Adam, shaking her hand warmly. "Would it be less trouble for you to invite her roommate, too — the pink-and-white inseparable?"

"No, thank you. I prefer to have Rebecca all to myself," said Miss Maxwell.

"I can understand that," replied Adam. "I mean, of course, that one girl is less trouble than two. There she is now."

Here Rebecca appeared in sight, walking down the quiet street with a boy of sixteen. They were in animated conversation and were apparently reading something aloud to each other, for the black head and the curly brown one were both bent over a sheet of letter paper. Rebecca kept glancing up at her companion, her eyes sparkling with appreciation.

"Miss Maxwell," said Adam merrily, "I am a trustee of this institution, but upon my word, I don't believe in coeducation!"

"I have my own occasional hours of doubt," she answered, restraining her mirth. "But surely its disadvantages are reduced to a minimum with youth like Rebecca! That is a very impressive sight which you are watching, Mr. Ladd. The folks at Harvard College were often privileged to view the famous poets, Longfellow and Lowell, walking together and reading to each other. The little school world of Wareham Academy palpitates with excitement when it sees the senior and the junior editors of *The Pilot* walking together!"

17

ROSES OF JOY

The day before Rebecca started for Nantucket Island with Miss Maxwell she was in the library with Emma Jane and Huldah, consulting dictionaries and encyclopedias. As they were leaving, they passed the cases containing the library of fiction. Rebecca's eyes fell upon a new book in the corner, and she read the name aloud with delight, "*Roses of Joy*. Listen girls; isn't that lovely? *Roses of Joy*. It looks beautiful, and it sounds beautiful. What does it mean, I wonder?" she remarked as they scampered together down the front steps. "Some day when I'm not so busy with my studies I shall check the book out and find out."

"I guess everybody has a different rose," said Huldah shrewdly. "I know what mine would be, and I'm not ashamed to admit it. I'd like to spend a year in Boston, with just as much money as I wanted to spend, horses and carriages and splendid clothes and amusement every minute of the day, and the theatre every evening of the week."

"That would be fun, for a while anyway," Emma Jane remarked. "But wouldn't that be pleasure more than joy? Oh, I've got an idea!"

"Don't shriek so!" said the startled Huldah. "I thought it was a mouse."

"I don't have them very often," apologized Emma Jane, "ideas, I mean. This one shook me like a stroke of lightning. Rebecca, couldn't one rose be success?"

"That's good," mused Rebecca. "I can see that success would be a joy, but it doesn't seem to me like a rose somehow. I was wondering if love might be a rose."

"I wish we had taken a peep at the book! It must be perfectly elergant!" said Emma Jane. "But now you say love; I think that's the best rose yet."

All day long the words "roses of joy" haunted and possessed Rebecca. She said them over to herself continually. Even Emma Jane was affected by them, for in the evening she said, "I have another idea—I had it while I was helping fix your hair. A rose of joy might be helpfulness."

"If it is, then roses are always blooming in your dear little heart, you darlingest, kind Emmie, taking such good care of your troublesome Becky!"

"Don't dare to call yourself troublesome! You're . . . you're . . . you're my special rose of joy, that's what you are!" And the two girls hugged each other affectionately.

In the middle of the night, Rebecca touched Emma Jane on the shoulder softly. "Are you very fast asleep, Emmie?" she whispered, seating herself lightly on the edge of Emma's bed.

"Not so very," answered Emma Jane drowsily.

"I've thought of something new. If you sang or painted or wrote—not a little, but beautifully, you know—wouldn't the doing of it, just as much as you wanted, give you a rose of joy?"

"It might if it was a real talent," answered Emma Jane, "though I don't like it so well as love. If you have another thought, Becky, keep it till morning."

"I did have one more inspiration," said Rebecca when they were dressing the next morning, "but I didn't wake you. I wondered if a rose of joy could be sacrifice? But I think sacrifice would be a lily, not a rose, don't you?"

◆ ◆ ◆

The train journey southward to Cape Cod and Nantucket, the first glimpse of the ocean, the steamer ride to the island, the strange new scenes, the ease and delicious freedom, the times of quiet talks with Miss Maxwell, almost intoxicated Rebecca. In three days she was not only herself again, she was another self, thrilling with delight, anticipation, and realization. She had always had such an eager hunger for knowledge, such a thirst for love, such a passionate longing for the music, the beauty, the poetry of existence! She had always been straining to make the outward world conform to her inward dreams, and now life had grown all at once rich and sweet, wide and full.

Rebecca was using all her natural, God-given outlets, and Emily Maxwell marveled daily at the inexhaustible way in which the girl poured out and gathered in the treasures of thought and experience that belonged to her. She was a lifegiver, altering the whole scheme of any picture she became a part of by contributing new values. Have you ever seen the dull blues and greens of a shaded room changed, transfigured by a burst of sunshine? That seemed to Miss Maxwell the effect of Rebecca on the groups of people with whom they now and then mingled. But they were usually alone, reading to each other and having happy talks.

Too, the prize essay was very much on Rebecca's mind. Secretly she thought she could never be happy unless she won it. She cared nothing for the value of it, and in this case almost nothing for the honor. She wanted to please Mr. Aladdin and Miss Maxwell and justify their belief in her.

Miss Maxwell and Rebecca were sitting by a little brook near the ocean on a sunny spring day. They had been in a stretch of wood by the sea since breakfast, going every now and then for a bask on the warm white sand and returning to their shady solitude when tired of the sun's glare.

"If I ever succeed in choosing a subject," remarked Rebecca, "I must ask if you think I can write well on it. Then I suppose I must work in silence and secret, never even reading the essay to you, nor talking about it."

"The subject *is* very important," said Miss Maxwell, "but I do not dare choose for you. Have you decided on anything yet?"

"No," Rebecca answered. "I plan a new essay every night. I've begun one on 'What is a Failure?' and another on 'He and She.' That would be a dialogue between a boy and girl just as they were leaving school and would tell their ideals of life. Then do you remember you said to me one day, 'Follow your mentor'? I'd love to write about that. I didn't have a single thought in Wareham, and now I have a new one every minute, so I must try and write the essay here. I shall think it out, at any rate, while I am so happy and free and rested. Look at the pebbles in the bottom of the pool, Miss Emily, so round and smooth and shining."

"Yes, but where did they get that beautiful polish, that satin skin, that lovely shape, Rebecca? Not in the still pool lying on the sands. It was never there that their angles were rubbed off and their rough surfaces polished, but in the strife and warfare of running waters. They have jostled against other pebbles, dashed against sharp rocks, and now we look at them and call them beautiful."

"If Fate had not made somebody a teacher, She might have been, oh, such a splendid preacher!" rhymed Rebecca. "Oh, if I could only think and speak as you do!" she sighed. "I am so afraid I shall never get education enough to make a good writer."

"You could worry about plenty of other things to better advantage," said Miss Maxwell a little scornfully. "Be afraid, for instance, that you won't understand human nature, that you won't realize the beauty of the outer world, or that you may lack sympathy, and, thus, never be able to read a heart. Fear that your faculty of expression may not keep pace with your ideas—a thousand things, every one of them more important to the writer than the knowledge that is found in books. Aesop was a Greek slave who could not even write down his wonderful fables—yet all the world reads them."

"I didn't know that," said Rebecca delighted. "I didn't know anything until I met you!"

"You will only have had a high-school education, yet even the most famous universities do not always succeed in building men and women. When I long to go to Europe and study, I always remember that there were three great schools in Athens and two in Jerusalem. But the Teacher of all teachers came out of a carpenter's shop in Nazareth, a little village hidden away from the bigger, busier world."

"Mr. Ladd says that you are almost wasted on Wareham," said Rebecca thoughtfully.

"He is wrong. My talent is not great, but no talent is wholly wasted unless its owner chooses to hide it in a napkin. Remember that of your own gifts, Rebecca. They may not be praised of men, but they may cheer, console, inspire others, perhaps when and where you least expect. The brimming glass that overflows its own rim moistens the earth about it."

"Now I'm going to give you the fir pillow. And while you take a nap, I am going down on the beach and write a story for you," said Rebecca. "It's one of my 'supposing' kind. It makes beautiful things happen that may never really all come to pass. But some of them will—you'll see! And then one day you'll take out my little story from your desk and remember Rebecca."

I wonder why these young things always choose subjects that would tax the powers of a great essayist! thought Miss Maxwell as she tried to sleep. *Are they dazzled, captivated, taken possession of, by the splendor of the theme, and do they fancy they can write up to it? Poor little innocent, hitching her tiny wagon to the stars! How pretty this particular innocent looks under her new parasol!*

Adam Ladd had been driving through Boston streets on a cold spring day one week before Rebecca and Emily Maxwell had left for Nantucket. Suddenly he spied a rose-colored parasol prettily unfurled in a shop window, signaling the passerby and setting him to dream of summer sunshine. It reminded Adam of a New England apple tree in full bloom—the outer covering of deep pink shining through the thin, white lining and a fluffy, fringe-like edge of mingled rose and cream dropping over the green handle. All at once he remembered one of Rebecca's early tales of woe—her little pink sunshade that had given her the only peep into the gay world of fashion that her childhood had ever known, her adoration of her flimsy bit of finery and its tragic end, ruined by a rain shower that had so rusted the frame that it soiled the fabric. He entered the shop, bought the extravagant parasol, and sent it by express delivery to Wareham at once, not a single doubt of its appropriateness crossing the darkness of his masculine mind. He thought only of the joy in Rebecca's eyes, of the poise of her head under the apple-blossom canopy. He was a trifle embarrassed to return an hour later and buy a blue parasol for Emma Jane Perkins, but it seemed increasingly difficult, as the years went on, to remember her existence at all the proper times and seasons.

This is Rebecca's story, recopied the next day and given to Emily Maxwell just as she was going to her room for the night. She read it with tears in her eyes and then sent it to Adam Ladd, thinking he had earned a share in it and deserved a glimpse of the girl's budding imagination, as well as of her grateful young heart.

A Fairy Story

There was once a tired and rather poverty-stricken Princess who dwelt in a cottage on the great highway between the City of Mansoul and the City of the King. She was not unhappy, like thousands of others. Truly she had much to be grateful for, but the life she lived and the work she did were hard indeed for one who was so small and tender.

Now the Princess' cottage stood by the edge of a great green forest where the wind was always singing in the branches and the sunshine filtering through the leaves. And one day when she was sitting by the wayside quite spent by her labor in the fields, she saw a golden chariot rolling down the King's Highway and in it a person who could be none other than somebody's Fairy Godmother on her way to the court. The chariot halted at her door, and though the Princess had read of such beneficent personages, she never dreamed for an instant that one of them could ever alight at her little cottage.

"If you are tired, poor little Princess, why do you not go into the cool green forest and rest?" asked the Fairy Godmother.

"Because I have no time," she answered. "I must go back to my plow."

"Is that your plow leaning by the tree, and is it not heavy?"

"It is heavy," answered the Princess, "but I love to turn the hard earth into soft furrows and know that I am making good soil wherein my seeds may grow. When I feel the weight too much and my shoulders ache, I try to think of the harvest."

The golden chariot passed on, and the two talked no more together that day. Nevertheless, the King's messengers were busy, for they whispered one word into the ear of the Fairy Godmother and another into the ear of the Princess, though so faintly that neither of them realized that the King had spoken.

The next morning a strong man knocked at the cottage door, and tipping his hat to the Princess he said, "A golden chariot passed me yesterday, and a passenger within it flung me a gold-clasped Book, and in the Book I read, 'Go out into the King's Highway and search until you find a cottage with a heavy plow leaning against a tree nearby. Enter and say to the Princess whom you will find there, "I will guide the plow and you must go and rest or walk in the cool green forest, for this is the command of your Fairy Godmother."'"

And the same thing happened every day. And every day the tired Princess walked in the green wood. Many times she caught the glitter of the chariot and ran into the King's Highway to give thanks to the Fairy Godmother, but she was never fleet enough to reach the spot. She could only stand with eager eyes and longing heart as the chariot passed by. Yet she never failed to catch a smile, and sometimes a word or two floated back to her, words that sounded like, "I would not be thanked. We can all become children of the same King, and I am only his messenger."

Now as the Princess walked daily in the green forest, hearing the wind singing in the branches and seeing the sunlight filter through the latticework of green leaves, there came unto her thoughts that had lain asleep in the stifling air of her cottage and in the weariness of guiding the plow. And by and by she took a needle from her girdle and pricked the thoughts onto the leaves of the trees and sent them into the air to float here and there.

And it came to pass that people began to pick them up, and holding them against the sun, they began to read what was written on them. And this because her simple little words on the leaves were only, after all, a part of one of the King's messages written on pages from the golden Book, such as the Fairy Godmother dropped continually from her golden chariot.

But the miracle of the story lies deeper than all this.

Whenever the Princess pricked the words upon the leaves, she added a thought of her Fairy Godmother, and folding it close within, sent the leaf out on the breeze to float here and there and fall where it would. And many other princesses felt the same impulse and did the same thing. And as nothing is ever lost in the King's dominion, so these thoughts and wishes and hopes, being full of love and gratitude, had no power to die, but take unto themselves other shapes and live on forever, for they return always to the King who first breathed them. They cannot be seen, our vision is too weak, nor heard, our hearing is too dull. But they can sometimes be felt, and we know that it is the King's influence that is stirring our hearts to nobler aims.

The end of the story is not come, but it may be that someday when the Fairy Godmother has a message to deliver in person straight to the King, he will say, "Your face I know. Your voice, your thoughts, and your heart I know also. I have heard the rumble of your chariot wheels on the Great Highway, and I knew that you were on the King's business. Here in my hand is a sheaf of messages from every quarter of my kingdom. They were delivered by weary and footsore travelers who said that they could never have reached the gate of the City of the King in safety had it not been for your help and inspiration. Read them, that you may know when and where and how you sped the King's service."

And when the Fairy Godmother reads them, it may be that sweet odors will rise from the pages and half-forgotten memories will stir the air. But in the gladness of the moment, nothing will be half so lovely as the voice of the King when he says, "Read, and know how you sped the King's service."

Rebecca Randall

18

OVER THE TEACUPS

The spring semester at Wareham had ended, and Huldah Meserve, Dick Carter, and Ted Perkins had finished school, leaving Rebecca and Emma Jane to represent Riverboro in the year to come. Alice Robinson's aunt, Delia Weeks, was at home from Lewiston on a brief visit. Her sister, Mrs. Robinson, was celebrating Delia's visit by a small and select party, that particular day having been set aside because strawberries were ripe and there was an old rooster that needed killing. Mrs. Robinson explained this to her husband, and she requested that he eat his dinner on the carpenter's bench in the shed, as the party was going to be a ladies' affair.

"All right. It won't be any loss to me," said Hillard Robinson. "Give me a good plate of baked yelloweye beans, that's all I ask. When a rooster is to be killed, I want somebody else to eat him, not me!"

Mrs. Robinson had company only once or twice a year and was usually quite ill for several days afterward, since the struggle between her pride and her stinginess was too great a strain on her. To maintain her standing in the community, she felt it necessary to set a good table, yet the supposed extravagance of the preparations goaded her

from the first moment she began to stir the marble cake to
the final moment when the feast was set out for her guests.

The aged rooster had been boiling steadily over a slow
fire on the kitchen range since morning, but he was so
resilient that his shape was as firm and handsome in the
pot as at the moment he was lowered into it. "He ain't
goin' to give up!" said Alice, peering nervously under the
cover, "and he looks like a scarecrow."

"We'll see whether he gives up or not when I take a
sharp knife to him," her mother answered. "And as to his
looks, a platter full of gravy makes a sight of difference
with old roosters, and I'll put dumplings 'round the edge.
They're terrible fillin', though they don't belong with
boiled chicken."

The rooster did indeed make an impressive showing,
lying in his border of dumplings, and the dish was much
complimented when it was brought in by Alice. This was
fortunate, as the chorus of admiration ceased abruptly
when the ladies began to eat the elderly fowl.

"I was glad to get over to Huldah's graduation, Delia,"
said Mrs. Meserve, who sat at the foot of the table and
helped serve the chicken while Mrs. Robinson poured cof-
fee at the other end. She was a fit mother for Huldah,
being much the most stylish person in Riverboro. Ill health
and good dress were, indeed, her two chief enjoyments in
life. It was rumored that her elaborately curled wig had
cost five dollars and that she sent it to Portland twice a
year to be set and frizzed, but it is extremely difficult to
discover the precise facts in such cases.

As to Mrs. Meserve's appearance, have you ever as a
child hung around the kitchen table while your mother
rolled out sugar gingerbread? Perhaps then, in some moment of amiability, she made you a dough lady, cutting the
outline deftly with her pastry knife, then placing the

human stamp on it by sticking in two black raisins for
eyes. Just call to mind the face of that sugar gingerbread
lady and you will have an exact portrait of Huldah's
mother — Mrs. Peter Meserve, she was generally called.

"How'd you like Huldah's dress, Delia?" she asked,
snapping the elastic in her black bracelets after an irritating
habit she had.

"I thought it was the handsomest of any," answered
Delia, "and her composition was first rate. It was the only
really amusing one there was, and she read it so loud and
clear we didn't miss any of it. Most of the girls spoke as if
they had hasty puddin' in their mouths."

"That was the composition she wrote for Adam Ladd's
prize," explained Mrs. Meserve. "And they do say she'd
'a' come out first, 'stead o' fourth, if her subject had been
different. There were three ministers and three deacons on
the committee, and it was only natural that they should
choose a serious piece — hers was too lively to suit 'em."

Huldah's inspiring theme had been "Boys," and she
certainly had a fund of knowledge and experience that fitted her to write most intelligently upon it. It was vastly
popular with the audience, who enjoyed the rather cheap
jokes and allusions with which it glittered. But judged
from a purely literary standpoint, it left much to be desired.

"Rebecca's piece wasn't read out loud, but the boy's
piece that took the prize was. Why was that?" asked Mrs.
Robinson.

"Because she wasn't graduating," explained Mrs.
Cobb, who had got her knowledge of the matter from Miss
Maxwell first hand. "She couldn't take part in the exer-
cises. But it'll be printed in the school paper. She writ it
about 'The Soul and the Spirit in the Poetry of John
Donne,'" added Aunt Sarah Cobb, "but I can't say's I kin

remember readin' enny of Donne's poems when I was in school," she confessed.

"I'm glad of that, for I'll never believe it was better'n Huldah's till I read it with my own eyes. It seems as if the prize ought to 'a' gone to one of the seniors."

"Well, no, Martha, not if Ladd offered it to any of the two upper classes that wanted to try for it," argued Mrs. Robinson. "They say they asked him to give out the prizes, and he refused. It seems odd, his being so rich and traveling about all over the country, that he was too modest to get up on that platform."

"My Huldah could 'a' done it and not winked an eyelash," observed Mrs. Meserve complacently, a remark which no one present seemed disposed to dispute.

"It was complete, though, since the governor happened to be there to see his niece graduate," said Delia Weeks. "Land! he looked elegant! They say he's only six feet tall, but he might have been sixteen, and he certainly did make a fine speech."

"Did you notice Rebecca, how white she was, and how she trembled when she and Herbert Dunn stood there while the governor was praising 'em? He'd read her composition, too, for he wrote her aunts a letter about it." This remark was from the sympathetic Aunt Sarah Cobb.

"I thought twas kinda foolish, his makin' so much of her when it wa'n't her graduation," objected Mrs. Meserve. "Layin' his hand on her head an' all that, as if he was a minister pronouncin' the benediction. But there! I'm glad the prize came to a Riverboro student, at any rate, and a handsomer one never was given out from the Wareham Academy platform. I guess there ain't no end to Adam Ladd's money. The hundred dollars would have been good enough, but he must needs go and put it in those elegant purses."

"I sat so far back I couldn't see 'em well," complained Delia, "and now Rebecca has taken hers home to Sunnybrook Farm in Temperance to show her mother."

"It was kind of a gold net bag with a chain," said Mrs. Perkins, "and there were five twenty dollar gold pieces in it. Herbert Dunn's was put in a fine leather wallet."

"How long is Rebecca goin' to stay at the farm?" asked Delia. "Maybe a month," answered Mrs. Perkins. "She's got to be back in Riverboro by early July to take up her summer studies with the minister's wife. Now't Hannah's married, Becky is a great help at Sunnybrook puttin' in the spring crops. She kin drive a team of hosses jest as good's a man, my Bill sez."

"It seems as if Hannah might 'a' waited a little longer. Aurelia was set against her goin' away while Rebecca was at school. But she's obstinate as a mule, Hannah is, and she just took her own way in spite of her mother," put in Mrs. Meserve.

"Girls need a life of their own, sooner or later," Mrs. Perkins gently reminded her. "It's not sech a strain t' do without Hannah, now that Rebecca's brothers are nearly grown. But they *do* need extra help in plantin' an' harvest time."

"Don't they say there's a good chance of the railroad goin' through her place?" asked Mrs. Cobb. "If it does, she'll get paid as much for her farm as it's worth, and more. Adam Ladd's one of the stockholders, an' they voted him a director. Everything is a success he takes hold of. They're fightin' it in the state capitol, but I'd back Mr. Ladd against any one of them legislators if he believed he was in the right."

"Rebecca'll have some new clothes now," said Delia, "and the Lord knows she needs them. Seems to me the Sawyer girls are gettin' terribly tight with their money."

"Rebecca won't have any new clothes out of the prize money," remarked Mrs. Perkins, "for she sent it away the next day to pay the interest on that mortgage — *two years* interest, at that!"

"Poor little girl!" exclaimed Delia Weeks.

"She might as well help along her folks as spend it on foolishness," affirmed Mrs. Robinson. "I think she was mighty lucky to get it to pay the interest with, but she's probably like all the Randalls. It was easy come, easy go, with them."

"That's more'n can be said of the Sawyer side of the family," retorted Mrs. Perkins. "Seems like they enjoyed savin' more'n anything in the world, and it's gaining on Miranda since her stroke."

"I don't believe it was a stroke. It stands to reason she'd never 'a' got up after it and been so smart as she is now. We had three of the worst strokes in our family that there ever was on this river, and I know every symptom of 'em better'n the doctors." And Mrs. Peter Meserve shook her head wisely.

"Miranda's strong enough," said Mrs. Cobb, "but you notice she stays right to home, and she's more close-mouthed than she ever was. Never took a mite o' pride in Rebecca's prize, as far as I could see, though it pretty nigh drove my Jeremiah out of his senses. I thought I should 'a' died o' shame when he cried 'Hoorah!' an' swung his straw hat when the governor shook hands with Rebecca. It's lucky he couldn't get far into the church and had to stand back by the door, for as it was, he made a spectacle of himself. My suspicion is" — and here every lady stopped eating and sat up straight — "that the Sawyer girls have lost money. They don't know a thing about business and never did, and Miranda's too secretive and contrary to ask advice."

"The most of what they've got is in gov'munt bonds, I always heard, and you can't lose money on them. Jane had the timberland left her, an' Miranda had the fields and the brick house — the whole quarter-section o' land. She probably took it awful hard that Rebecca's hundred dollars had to be swallowed up in a mortgage, 'stead o' goin' toward school expenses. The more I think of it, the more I think Adam Ladd intended Rebecca should have that prize when he gave it." The mind of Huldah's mother ran toward the idea that her daughter's rights had been violated.

"Land, Martha, what foolishness you talk!" exclaimed Mrs. Perkins. "You don't suppose he could tell what composition the committee was going to choose. And why should he offer another hundred dollars for a boy's prize, if he wasn't interested in helpin' the school? He's given Emma Jane about the same present as Rebecca every Christmas for four years. That's the way he does things."

"Someday he'll forget one of them and give to the other, or drop 'em both and give to some new girl!" said Delia Weeks, with an experience born of fifty years of unmarried life.

"Like as not," agreed Mrs. Peter Meserve, "though it's easy to see he ain't the marryin' kind. There's men that would marry once a year if their wives would die fast enough, and there's men that seem to want to live alone."

"I guess Ladd could have any woman in Riverboro that's of suitable age, if he wanted her," pleasantly remarked Mrs. Perkins.

"'Tain't likely he could be caught by any Riverboro girl," demurred Mrs. Robinson. "Not when he probably has had his pick of the girls in Boston. I guess Martha hit it when she said there's men that ain't the marryin' kind."

"I wouldn't trust any of 'em when Miss Right comes along!" laughed Mrs. Cobb genially. "You never can tell what 'n' who's goin' to please 'em. You know Jeremiah's contrary horse, Buster? He won't let anybody put a bit into his mouth if he can help it. He'll fight Jerry and fight me till he has to give in.

"Rebecca didn't know nothin' about his tricks, an' the other day she went into the barn to hitch up that horse for Jerry. I followed right along, just *knowin'* she'd have trouble with the halter. And I declare if she wasn't pattin' Buster's nose an' talkin' to him. And when she put her little fingers into his mouth he opened it so far I thought he'd swaller her, fer sure. 'Land, Rebecca,' I says, 'how'd you persuade him to take the bit?'

"'I didn't,' she says. 'He seemed to want it. Perhaps he's tired of his stall and wants to get out in the fresh air.'"

19

SOLITUDE AT WAREHAM

Rebecca was sitting by the window in the room she shared with Emma Jane Perkins at Wareham Academy. She was alone, as Emma was poring over Latin below in some academic vault of the old brick building.

A new and most ardent passion for classic literature had been born in Emma Jane's brain, for Abijah Flagg, now a freshman at Bowdoin College, had written her a letter in Latin, a letter which, having failed that ancient language two years in a row, she had been unable to translate for herself, even with the aid of a dictionary. Emma had apparently been unwilling that Rebecca, her bosom friend, confidante, and roommate should translate it into English for her.

An old-fashioned boarding academy, with its allotment of one medium-sized room to two medium-sized young women, gave small opportunities for privacy night or day. Accordingly, like the irrational ostrich which defends itself by the simple process of not looking at its pursuers, Emma Jane had kept her Latin letter in her closed hand, in her pocket, or in her book, flattering herself that no one had noticed her pleased bewilderment at its only half-imagined contents.

All the fairies had not been present at Rebecca's birth cradle. A goodly number of them telegraphed that they were previously engaged or unavoidably absent from town. Sunnybrook Farm, near the village of Temperance, Maine, where Rebecca first saw the light of day, was hardly a place on its own merits to attract large throngs of fairies. But one dear old creature who keeps her pocket full of Merry Leaves from the Laughing Tree took a fancy to come to the little birthday party. Seeing so few of her sister fairies present, she dowered the sleeping baby more richly than usual because of the child's apparent lack of wealth in other directions.

So the child grew, and the Merry Leaves from the Laughing Tree rustled where they hung from the hood of her cradle. And being fairy leaves, when the cradle was given up, they festooned themselves on the cribside. And later on they blew themselves up to the ceilings at Sunnybrook Farm and dangled there, making fun for everybody. They never withered, even at the brick house in Riverboro, where the air was particularly hostile to fairies, for Miss Miranda Sawyer would have scared any ordinary elf out of her seventeen senses.

These fairies — or guardian angels, if you please — followed Rebecca to Wareham. During Abijah Flagg's Latin correspondence with Emma Jane, they fluttered about that young person's head in such a manner that Rebecca was almost afraid that Emma would discover them herself, although this is something, as a matter of fact, that never does happen.

A week had gone by since the Latin letter had been taken from her mail pigeonhole by Emma Jane. And now, by means of much midnight oil burning, by much cautious questioning of Miss Maxwell, by such scrutiny of the moods and tenses of Latin verbs as well-nigh destroyed her brain tissue, she had mastered its romantic message. The phrases and the sentiments, when finally translated and written down in black-and-white English, made, in Emma Jane's opinion, the most convincing and heart-melting document ever sent through the mail:

Mea Cara Emma:

Cur audeo scribere ad te epistulam? Es mihi dea! Semper es in mea anima. Iterum et iterum es cum me in somnis. Saepe video capillos auri, tuos pulchros oculos similes caelo, tuas genas, quasi rubentes rosas in nive. Tua vox est dulcior quam cantus avium aut murmur rivuli in montibus.

Cur sum ego tam miser et pauper et indignus, et tu tam dulcis et bona et noblis?

Si cogitabis de me ero beatus. Tu es sola puella quam amo et semper eris. Alias puellas non amavi. Forte olim amabis me, sed sum indignus. Sine to sum miser, cum tu es prope mea vita omnis est guadimm.

Vale, carissima, carissima puella!

De tuo fideli servo,

Abijah Flagg

My Dear Emma:

Why dare I write you a letter? You are to me a goddess!

Always you are on my heart. Again and again you are with me in dreams. Often I see your locks of gold, your beautiful eyes like the sky, your cheeks, as red as roses in snow. Your voice is sweeter than the singing of birds or the murmur of the stream in the mountains.

Why am I so wretched and poor and unworthy, and you so sweet and good and noble?

If you will think of me, I shall be happy. You are the only girl that I love and always will be. Other girls I have not loved. Perhaps sometime you will love me, but I am unworthy. Without you I am wretched. When you are near, my life is all joy.

Farewell dearest, dearest girl!

From your faithful slave,

Abijah Flagg

Emma Jane knew the letter by heart in English. She even knew it in Latin, which only a few days before had been a dead language to her, but now it was one filled with life and meaning. From beginning to end, the epistle had the effect upon her of an intoxicating elixir. Often, at morning prayers or while eating her rice pudding at the noon dinner or when sinking off to sleep at night, she heard a voice murmuring in her ear, *"Vale carissima, carissima puella!"*

As to the effect on her modest, countrified little heart of the phrases in which college boy Abijah stated she was a goddess and he her faithful slave, that quite baffles description. It lifted her bodily out of the scenes in which she moved into a new, rosy, ethereal atmosphere in which even Rebecca had no place.

Rebecca did not know this, fortunately. She only suspected and waited for the day when Emma Jane would pour out her confidences, as she always did and always would until the end of time. At the present moment, Rebecca was busily employed in thinking about her own affairs. A shabby composition book with mottled covers lay open on the table before her. Sometimes she wrote in it with feverish haste and absorption; sometimes she rested her chin in the cup of her palm, and with her pencil poised in the other hand, she looked dreamily out on Wareham Village below the campus — its huddle of roofs and steeples all blurred into positive beauty by the fast-falling snowflakes.

It was the middle of the December of Rebecca's senior year, and the friendly sky was softly dropping a great white mantle of peace and goodwill over the little town, making all ready within and without for the Feast of the Babe of Bethlehem.

The main street that in summer was dignified by its splendid avenue of majestic, goblet-shaped elm trees now ran quiet and white between rows of stalwart trunks, whose leafless branches were all hanging heavy under their dazzling white burden. The path leading straight up the hill to the academy was broken only by the feet of the hurrying, breathless boys and girls who ran up and down, carrying piles of books under their arms — books which they remembered so long as they were within the four walls of the recitation rooms and which they too often eagerly forgot as soon as they met one another in the living, laughing world, going up and down the hill.

"It's very becoming to the universe, snow is!" mused Rebecca, looking out of the window dreamily. "Really, there's too little to choose between the world and heaven when a snowstorm is going on. I feel as if I ought to look at it every minute. I wish I could get over being greedy, but it still seems to me at nearly seventeen as if there weren't enough waking hours of the day, and as if somehow I were pressed for time and continually losing something.

"How well I remember Mother's story about me when I was four. It was at early breakfast on the farm, but I called all meals 'dinner' then, and when I had finished, I folded up my bib and sighed, 'Oh dear! Only two more dinners, play a while and go to bed!' This was at six in the morning—lamplight in the kitchen, snowlight outside!

> Powdery, powdery, powdery snow,
> Making things lovely wherever you go!
> Merciful, merciful, merciful snow,
> Masking the ugliness hidden below.

"I must write a poem for the January *Pilot*, but I mustn't take the snow as a subject. There has been too much competition among the older poets!"

20

REBECCA'S
REMINISCENCES

A lone in her room, Rebecca turned in her chair and
began writing again in the shabby book, already
three-quarters filled with the scribblings of her childhood
hours, which she had hidden away in the barn loft of the
brick house so long ago. Sometimes these were in pencil
and sometimes in violet ink with carefully shaded capital
letters.

Rebecca wrote on the blank pages near the end as she
mused in her dorm room:

Abijah Flagg came back from Bowdoin College for the
Thanksgiving holiday last month. Thursday morning the
Burnham sisters from North Riverboro came over to
spend the day with Aunt Miranda at the brick house,
and Abijah went down there to put up their horse. He
scaled the ladder to the barn chamber—the dear old ladder that used to be my safety valve—and pitched down
the last forkful of grandfather's hay that will ever be
eaten by any visiting horse. They will be delighted to
hear that it is all gone. Every horse that has been a guest

at the brick house has complained about that hay for years and years.

What should Abijah find at the bottom of the heap of hay but my Thought Book, carelessly hidden there years ago and almost forgotten. I'm not sure whether I'm angry or glad that he discovered it. I suppose I shall never know if he peeked inside, but I do thank him for giving it to me promptly. Oh, if Aunt Miranda had seen it!

When I think of what this book was to me, the place it filled in my life, the affection I lavished on it, I wonder that I could forget it, even in all the excitement of coming to Wareham to school. And that gives me an "uncommon thought," as I used to say. It is this: when we finish building an air castle, we seldom live in it after all. We sometimes even forget that we ever longed to! Perhaps we have gone so far as to begin to build another castle on a higher hilltop. And this is so beautiful—especially while we are building and before we live in it—that the first one has quite vanished from sight and mind, like the outgrown shell of the nautilus that he casts off on the shore and never looks at again. At least I suppose he doesn't. But perhaps he takes one backward glance, half smiling, half serious, just as I am doing at my old Thought Book, and he says, "Was that ever my shell? Goodness gracious, how did I ever squeeze myself into it?"

That bit about the nautilus sounds like an extract from a school theme or a *Pilot* editorial or a fragment of one of dear Miss Maxwell's lectures—was it from Holmes? I think at almost seventeen I am principally an imitator of the people and things I love and admire. Between editing *The Pilot*, writing out Virgil translations from Latin, searching for composition subjects, and studying rhetorical models, there is very little of the original Rebecca

*Alone in her room, Rebecca turned in her chair
and began writing again in the shabby book.*

Rowena about me at the present moment. I am just a member of the graduating class in good and regular standing. We do our hair alike, dress alike as much as possible, eat and drink alike, talk alike, even. I am not even sure that we do not think alike. And what will become of the poor world when we are all let loose upon it on the same day next June? Will life, real life, bring our true selves back to us? Will love and duty and sorrow and trouble and work finally wear off the school stamp that has been pressed upon all of us until we look like rows of shining copper cents fresh from the mint?

Yet there must be a little difference between us somewhere, or why does Abijah Flagg write Latin letters to Emma Jane instead of to me? There is one example on the other side of the argument — Abijah Flagg. He stands out from all the rest of the boys like the Rock of Gibraltar on the calendar pictures. Is it because he never went to school until he began college at twenty? He almost died of longing to go to school, and the longing seemed to teach him more than the going.

Abijah knew his letters, and he could read simple things, but it was I who taught him what books really meant when I was twelve and he sixteen. We studied while he was husking corn or cutting potatoes for seed or shelling yelloweyes with his flail in the squire's barn. His beloved Emma Jane didn't teach him — her father would not permit her to be friends with a chore boy! It was I who found him after milking time on summer nights, suffering, yes dying, of least common multiple and greatest common divisor. I who struck the shackles from the slave and told him to skip it all and go on to something easier like fractions, percentages, and compound interest, as I did myself. Oh, how he used to smell of the cows when I was correcting his sums on warm evenings! But I don't regret it, for he is now

doing well at Bowdoin, and he is the pride of Riverboro.
I suppose he even has forgotten the proper side on
which to approach a cow if you wish to milk her. This
now unserviceable knowledge is neatly enclosed in the
outgrown shell he threw off a year ago.

Abijah's gratitude to me knows no bounds, but he writes
Latin letters to Emma Jane! But as Mrs. Perkins said (I
now quote from myself at thirteen), "It is the way of the
world and how things have to be!"

Well, I have read my old Thought Book all through, and
when I want to make Mr. Aladdin laugh, I shall show
him my composition on the relative values of punishment and reward as builders of character.

I am not at all the same Rebecca Rowena Randall today
that I was then, at twelve, thirteen, or fourteen. I hope,
in getting rid of my failings, that I haven't scrubbed and
rubbed so hard that I have taken the gloss off the poor
little virtues that lay just alongside of the faults. For as I
read the foolish doggerel and the funny, funny
"Remerniscences," I see on the whole a nice, well-
meaning, trusting, loving, heedless little creature, that
after all, I'd rather build on than outgrow altogether, because she is Me — the Me that was made and born just a
little different from all the rest of the babies in my birthday year.

One thing is alike in the child and the girl. They both
love to set thoughts down in black and white to see how
they look, how they sound, and how they make one feel
when one reads them over. They both love the sound of
beautiful sentences and the tinkle of rhyming words, and
in fact, of the three great R's of life. They adore Reading and 'Riting as much as they abhor 'Rithmetic.

The little girl in the old book is always thinking of what
she is "going to be." Uncle Jerry Cobb spoiled me a

good deal in this direction. I remember he said to everybody when I wrote my verses for the flag raising, "Nary rung on the ladder o' fame but that child'll climb if you give her time!" Poor Uncle Jerry! He will be so disappointed in me as time goes on. And still he would think I have already climbed two rungs on the ladder, although it is only a little Wareham ladder, for I am *The Pilot's* editor, the first girl editor — and I have taken a hundred-dollar prize in composition and paid two years' interest on a twelve-hundred-dollar mortgage with it.

> High is the rank we now possess,
> But higher we shall rise:
> Though what we shall hereafter be
> Is hid from mortal eyes.

This hymn was sung in church the Sunday after my election to editor, and Mr. Aladdin was there that day and looked across the aisle and smiled at me. Then he sent me a sheet of paper from Boston the next morning with just one verse in the middle of it:

> She made the cleverest people ashamed;
> And ev'n the good with inward envy groan,
> Finding themselves so very much exceeded,
> In their own way by all the things
>   that she did.

Miss Maxwell says it is Byron, and I wish I had thought of the last rhyme before Byron did — my rhymes are always so common.

I am too busy doing, nowadays, to give very much thought to being. Mr. Aladdin was teasing me one day about what he calls my "cast-off careers."

"What makes you aim at any mark in particular, Rebecca?" he asked, looking at Miss Maxwell and laughing. "Women never hit what they aim at, anyway. But if they shut their eyes and shoot in the air they generally find themselves in the bull's eye."

I think one reason that I have always dreamed of what I should be when I grew up is that even before Father died Mother worried about the mortgage on the farm and what would become of us if it were foreclosed. It was hard on the children to be brought up with a mortgage that way. But, oh, it was harder still on poor, dear Mother, who had seven of us then to think of, and still has three at home to feed and clothe out of the farm.

Aunt Jane says I am young for my age. Aunt Miranda is afraid that I will never really grow up. Mr. Aladdin says that I don't know the world any better than the pearl inside of the oyster knows the sea. They none of them know the old, old thoughts I have, some of them going back years and years, for these thoughts are never ones I could speak about.

I remember how we children used to admire Father. He was so handsome and graceful and amusing, never cross like Mother, or too busy to play with us. He never did much work around the house because he had to keep his hands nice for playing the church organ or the violin or the piano. Mother used to say, "Hannah and Rebecca, you must hull the strawberries; your father cannot help. John, you must milk the cow for I haven't the time and it would spoil your father's hands."

All the other men in Temperance Village wore plaid or flannel shirts, except on Sundays. But Father never wore any but starched white ones. He was very particular about them, and Mother used to stitch and stitch on the pleats, and press and press the collar and cuffs, sometimes late at night. Father did most of his work in his white shirts, for when he was not teaching boys to play the violin and girls to sing and play the piano, he was busy in his accounts. Had he made his books balance as well as he could sing and play, Mother would not now have a mortgage on Sunnybrook Farm!

As I look back, I see that Miss Ross, the artist who brought me my pink parasol from Paris, sowed the first seeds in me of ambition to do something special. Her life seemed so beautiful and so easy to a child. I had not been to school then or read George MacDonald, so I did not know that "Ease is the lovely result of forgotten toil."

Miss Ross sat out of doors and painted lovely things, and everybody said how wonderful they were and bought them straightway immediately. And she supported her blind father and two brothers and traveled wherever she wished. It comes back to me now, that summer when I was ten and Miss Ross painted me sitting by the mill wheel while she talked to me of foreign countries!

The other day Miss Maxwell read something from Browning's poems to her literature class. It was about David the shepherd boy who used to lie in his valley watching one eagle "wheeling slow as in sleep." He used to wonder about the wide world that the eagle beheld outside his valley, the eagle that was stretching his wings up so far in the blue while he, the poor shepherd boy, could see only the "strip 'twixt the hill and the sky," for he lay in a narrow valley between high mountains.

I told Mr. Baxter about it the next day, which was the Saturday before I joined the church. I asked him if it was wicked to long to see as much as the eagle saw.

There was never anybody quite like Reverend Baxter. "Rebecca dear," he said, "it may be that you need not always lie in a valley, as the shepherd boy did. But wherever you lie, that little strip you see ''twixt the hill and the sky' is able to hold all of earth and all of heaven, if only you have the right sort of vision. Keep your eyes fixed on Jesus and read daily in His Word."

It seems like it took me a long time to understand about salvation, though Mother read the Bible to us from the earliest I can remember. I recall Sunday afternoons at the brick house the first winter after I went there, when I used to sit in the middle of the dining room as I was bid, silent and still, with the big family Bible on my knees.

Aunt Jane used to read the *Pilgrim's Progress*. The fire burned low; the tall clock ticked, ticked, so slowly and steadily that the pictures in the old Bible swam before my eyes and I almost fell asleep.

My aunts thought that by shutting everything else out I should see God. But I didn't, not once. I was so homesick for Sunnybrook and John that I could hardly learn my weekly hymns and Bible verses.

It was brother John for whom I was chiefly homesick on Sunday afternoons, because at Sunnybrook Farm, Father was dead and Mother was always busy and Hannah never liked to talk.

But God found me when He was ready, that evening when I ran away from Aunt Miranda to Uncle Jerry Cobb. Not all the religion of Aunt Miranda or the piety of Aunt Jane could open my heart to Jesus—but I am sure that their prayers were heard in heaven; God can understand old aunts if little nieces can't. Truly His ways are "past finding out."

Then the missionaries from Africa came to Riverboro, and at the meeting Mr. Burch saw me playing the church organ. I invited him and his family to spend the

night with us at the brick house, because Grandfather
Israel Sawyer used to invite the missionaries to stay
there. As things turned out, though Aunt Miranda was
angry with me for this at first, it did more for her religion than all her years of attending missionary society
meetings.

The year is nearly over, and the next few months will be
lived in the rush and whirlwind of work that comes before graduation. The bell for philosophy class will ring
in ten minutes, and as I have been writing for nearly
two hours, I must learn my lesson going up Academy
Hill. It will not be the first time — it is a grand hill for
learning! I suppose after fifty years or so the very
ground has become soaked with knowledge, and every
particle of air in the vicinity is crammed with useful information.

I will put my book into my trunk — having no blessed
haymow hereabouts — and take it out again — shall I ever
take it out again? Perhaps I shall hide it behind the
beam in the loft when I go home to the brick house for
Christmas and not be so careless as to leave it where it
can be found again — albeit under a pile of hay!

After graduation perhaps I shall be too grown up and
too busy to write in my Thought Book. But, oh, if only
something would happen worth putting down — something strange, something unusual, something different
from the things that happen every day in Riverboro and
Temperance!

Graduation will surely take me a little out of "the valley" — make me a little more like the soaring eagle, gaz-
ing at the whole wide world beneath him while he
wheels "slow as in sleep." But whatever happens I'll try
not to be a discontented shepherd but remember what
Pastor Baxter said, that the strip that I see "'twixt the

hill and the sky' is able to hold all of earth and all of heaven, if only I have eyes to see it.

Rebecca Rowena Randall
Wareham Academy
December 19th

21

GRADUATION
AT WAREHAM

A year had passed since Adam Ladd's prize had been
discussed over the teacups in Riverboro. The months
had come and gone, and at last the great day had dawned
for Rebecca — the day to which she had been looking forward for several years as the first grand goal to be reached
on her little journey through the world. School days were
ended, and her graduation was about to be celebrated; it
was even now heralded by the sun dawning on the eastern
sky.

Rebecca stole softly out of bed, slipped to the window,
threw open the blinds, and welcomed the rosy light that
meant a cloudless spring morning. Even the sun looked
different somehow — larger, redder, more important than
usual. And if the sun really were more beautiful, there was
no member of Rebecca's graduating class who would have
thought it strange in view of all the circumstances.

Emma Jane stirred on her pillow, woke, and seeing Rebecca at the window, came and knelt on the floor beside
her. "It's going to be pleasant, thank the Lord," she sighed
gratefully. "Did you sleep?"

"Not much. The words of my class poem kept running through my head, and the accompaniments of the songs."

No one who is unfamiliar with life in rural New England toward the end of the nineteenth century can imagine the gravity, the importance, the solemnity of this last day of school. In the matter of preparation, wealth of detail, and general excitement, it far surpasses a wedding, for that is commonly a simple affair in a Maine country village.

Nothing quite equals graduation in the minds of the graduates themselves, their families, and the younger students, unless it be the inauguration of a governor at the state capitol in Augusta. Wareham, then, was shaken to its very center on this day of days. Mothers and fathers of the students, as well as relatives, had been coming on the train and driving into the town in buggies and surries since breakfast time. Alumni and old students, both married and single, streamed back to the dear old village.

The village's two livery stables were crowded with vehicles of every sort. Lines of buggies and wagons were drawn up along the sides of the elm-shaded roads, the horses switching their tails in luxurious idleness as they munched oats from their nose bags. The streets were filled with people wearing their best clothes, and the fashions included not only the latest thing, but the well-preserved relic of a bygone day. There were all sorts and conditions of men and women, for there were sons and daughters of storekeepers, lawyers, ministers, statesmen, businessmen, millionaires, and farmers at Wareham Academy, either as boarders or day students.

In the academy dormitories, there was an excitement so profound that it expressed itself in a kind of hushed silence, a transient suspension of life, as those most interested approached the crucial moment. The feminine graduates-to-be were seated in their own bedrooms, dressed with a completeness of detail to which all their past lives seemed to have been but a prelude. At least this was the case with their bodies.

Their heads, however, because of the extreme heat of the day, were ornamented with lead curlers or papers or dozens of little braids, which when undone would issue in every sort of curl known to the girl of that period. Rolling the hair on leads or papers was a favorite method of attaining the desired result. And though it often entailed a sleepless night, there were those who gladly paid the price. Others, in whose being the blood of martyrs did not flow, substituted rags for leads and pretended that they made a more natural and less wooly curl.

But since heat will melt the proudest head and reduce to fiddle strings the finest product of the curling iron, anxious mothers were stationed over their daughters, waving palm leaf or Chinese rice paper fans. It had been decided that the instant when the town clock struck ten should be the time chosen for releasing the prisoners from their self-imposed tortures.

Dotted or plain swiss muslin was the favorite material for graduation dresses, though there were those who were steaming in white cashmere or alpaca, because in some cases such gowns were thought more useful afterward. Blue and pink waist ribbons were lying over the backs of chairs, and the girl who had a fine Roman sash was praying that she might be kept from vanity and pride.

But the way to any graduating dress at all had not seemed clear to Rebecca until a month before. Then with Emma Jane she visited the Perkins' attic where the girls had found, amongst goods left over from Emma's grandfather's general merchandise store, piece after piece of white cheesecloth. And they decided that, in a pinch, it would do. So Emma, the "rich blacksmith's daughter," cast the thought of dotted swiss behind her and elected to follow Rebecca in cheesecloth as she had in higher matters. Soon the girls were devising costumes that included such drawing of threads, such hemstitching and pin-tucking, such insertions of fine thread tatting that, to be finished on time, Rebecca's dress was given out in sections — the sash was sent by the postman to Hannah, waist and sleeves to Mrs. Cobb, and skirt to Aunt Jane. The stitches that went into the cheap material, worth only three or four pennies a yard, made the dresses altogether lovely. Satin or brocade, in fact, could not have been more beautiful.

The girls were waiting in their dorm room alone, and Emma Jane was in a rather tearful state of mind. She kept remembering that it was the last sweet day that they would be together. Emma Jane would not graduate, and since she had failed Latin and done badly in history, she elected, with Rebecca, to end her studies after three years.

For Rebecca, the beginning of the end seemed to have dawned, for two career opportunities had been offered her by Mr. Morrison the day before. In one, at Augusta, she would play for singing and calisthenics, and teach piano for the younger girls in a boarding school. The other was an assistant's place in Edgewood High School, only a dozen miles from Riverboro. Both were very modest as to salary, but the position at Augusta included educational advantages that Miss Maxwell thought might be valuable.

Rebecca's mood had passed from that of excitement into a sort of exaltation. And when the first bell rang through the corridors announcing that in five minutes the class would proceed together through Main Street to First Church for the exercises, she stood motionless and speechless at the window with her hand on her heart.

"It is coming, Emmie," she said presently. "Do you remember in *The Mill on the Floss,* when Maggie Tulliver closed the golden gates of childhood behind her? I can almost see them swing, almost hear them clang, and I can't tell whether I am glad or sorry."

"I shouldn't care how they swung or clanged," said Emma Jane plaintively, "if only you and I were on the same side of the gate. But we shan't be—I know we shan't!"

"Emmie, don't you dare cry, for I'm just on the brink of crying myself! If only you were graduating with me— that's my sorrow! There! I hear the church bell! People will be seeing our grand surprise soon now! Hug me once for luck, dear Emmie. Make it a careful hug, remembering our cheesecloth dresses!"

Ten minutes later, Adam Ladd, who had just arrived from Portland and was walking toward First Church, came suddenly into Wareham's Main Street and stopped short under a maple by the wayside, riveted to the spot by a scene of picturesque loveliness such as his eyes had never witnessed before. No class of which Rebecca was president was likely to follow accepted customs. Instead of marching two by two from the dorm to the church, they had elected to proceed there by royal chariot. A hay wagon had been decked with green vines and branches of long-stemmed field daisies, those gay darlings of New England meadows. Every inch of the wagon's rail, the body, even the spokes of its high wooden wheels, all were twined with yellow and green and white. There were two white horses with flower-trimmed reins, and in this floral bower, seated on maple boughs, were the twelve girls of the class, while the ten boys marched on either side of the vehicle, wearing buttonhole bouquets of daisies, the class flower.

Rebecca drove the horses herself, seated grandly on a green-covered bench that looked like a throne for the goddess of spring. No girl clad in white, flowing gown, no happy girl of seventeen is plain. And the twelve country maids, from the vantage of their setting, looked beautiful, as the June sunlight filtered down on their uncovered heads, showing their bright eyes, their fresh cheeks, their smiles, and their dimples.

Rebecca, Adam thought, as he took off his hat and saluted the pretty parade — Rebecca, with her tall slenderness, her thoughtful brow, the fire of young joy in her face, with her narrow band of dark, braided hair tied over her flowing, raven tresses, might have been a young Muse or Sibyl. And the flowery hayrack with its freight of blooming girlhood might have been painted as an allegorical picture of "The Morning of Life." It all passed him as he stood under the elms in the old village street where his mother had walked nearly thirty years before.

Adam turned to follow the crowd toward the church when he heard a little sob. Behind a hedge in the garden near where he was standing was a forlorn person in white, whose neat nose, chestnut hair, and blue eyes he knew well. He stepped inside the gate and said, "What's wrong, Miss Emma?"

"Oh, is it you, Mr. Ladd? Rebecca wouldn't let me cry for fear of spoiling my looks, but I must have just one good bawl before I go in. I can be as homely as I like, after all, for I only have to sing with the school choir. I'm not graduating; I'm just leaving, for I couldn't learn Latin and I flunked history. Not that I mind that. It's only being separated from Rebecca that I can never stand!"

The two walked along together, Adam comforting the disconsolate Emma Jane, until they reached the stately old meetinghouse where the commencement exercises were always held. The interior, with its decorations of yellow, green, and white, was crowded, the air hot and breathless, the essays and songs and recitations precisely like all others that have been since the world began.

Though we may yawn desperately at the essays, our hearts go out to the graduating essayists all the same, for "the vision splendid" is shining in their eyes, and there is no fear of the yoke of adult responsibility that the years are so surely bringing them.

Rebecca saw her sister, Hannah, with her husband, Will, and their new baby in the audience. Dear brother John and cousin Ann were there also. She felt a pang at the absence of her mother, though she had known there was no possibility of seeing her. Poor Aurelia Randall was kept at Sunnybrook by cares of children and farm and by lack of money, either for the journey or for a suitable new dress.

The Cobbs she saw there, too. No one, indeed, could fail to see Uncle Jerry, for he shed tears more than once, and in the intervals between the essays, he boasted to those seated near him of the marvelous gifts of one of the graduating class whom he had known ever since she was a child. In fact, he had driven her from Maplewood to Riverboro when she left her home, and he had told Mother Cobb that same night that there wasn't nary a rung on the ladder of fame that that child wouldn't mount before she got through with it.

The Cobbs, then, had come, and there were other Riverboro faces. But where was Aunt Jane in her black silk, made over especially for this occasion? Aunt Miranda had not intended to come, she knew, but where, on this day of days was her beloved Aunt Jane? However, this thought, like all others, came and went in a flash, for the whole morning was like a series of magic-lantern pictures, crossing and recrossing her field of vision.

Rebecca played, she sang, she recited like one in a dream, only brought to consciousness by meeting Mr. Aladdin's eyes as she spoke the last line. Then at the end of the program came her class poem, "Makers of Tomorrow." And there, as on many former occasions, her personality played so great a part that she seemed to be uttering Miltonic sentiments instead of schoolgirl verse. Her voice, her eyes, her body breathed conviction, earnestness, and emotion, and when Rebecca left the platform the audience felt that they had listened to a masterpiece.

Most of her hearers knew little of Carlyle or Emerson, or they might have remembered that the one said, "We are all poets when we read a poem well," and the other, "'Tis the good reader makes the good book."

It was over! The diplomas had been presented, and each girl, after giving furtive touches to hair, sly tweaks to her muslin skirts, and caressing pats to her sash, had gone forward to receive the roll of parchment with a bow that had been the subject of anxious thought for weeks. Rounds of applause greeted each graduate as she took her diploma, saluted the principal with a curtsy, and returned to her seat. Jeremiah Cobb's behavior when Rebecca came forward was the talk of Wareham and Riverboro for days. Old Mrs. Webb avowed that he, in the space of two hours, had worn out the pew more — the carpet, the cushion, and woodwork — than she had by forty years of church attendance. Yes, it was over, and after the crowd had thinned a little, Adam Ladd made his way to the platform.

Rebecca turned from speaking to some strangers and met him in the aisle. "Oh, Mr. Aladdin," she said with a lilt in her voice, "I am so glad you could come! Tell me" — and she looked at him half shyly, for his approval was dearer to her than that of any of the others — "tell me, Mr. Aladdin — were you satisfied?"

"More than satisfied!" he said. "Glad I met the child, proud I know the girl, longing to meet the woman!"

With an impulse born of feelings which she scarcely recognized, Rebecca encircled his neck with her slender arms and kissed his cheek.

22

THE ROAD BEYOND

Her heart beating high from the sweet congratulation from her hero's lips, and blushing at the realization of her own impulsive behavior, Rebecca sought words to respond to Mr. Ladd's praise. But before she had found words to thank him, Mr. and Mrs. Cobb, who had been modestly biding their time in a corner, approached her, and she introduced them to Mr. Ladd.

"Where is Aunt Jane?" she cried, holding Aunt Sarah's hand on one side and Uncle Jerry's on the other.

"I'm sorry, but we've got bad news for you."

"Is Aunt Miranda worse? She is! I can see it by your looks." And Rebecca's color faded.

"She had a second stroke yesterday morning just when she was helpin' Jane lay out her things to come here today. Jane said you weren't to know anything about it till the graduatin' exercises were over, and we promised to keep it a secret till then."

"I will go right home with you, Aunt Sarah. I must run tell Miss Maxwell, for after I had packed up tomorrow, I was going over to Bowdoin College in Brunswick with her. Poor Aunt Miranda! And I have been so happy all day, except that I was longing to see Mother and Aunt Jane."

"There ain't no harm in bein' happy, dear," said Aunt Sarah. "That's what Jane wanted you to be. And Miranda's got her speech back, for your aunt has just sent a note sayin' she's better. I'm goin' to set up with Miranda tonight, so you can stay here and have a good sleep and get your things together comfortably tomorrow."

"I'll pack your trunk for you, Becky dear, and take care of all our room things," said Emma Jane who had come toward the group and heard the sorrowful news from the aunts at the brick house.

They moved into one of the quiet side pews of the chapel, where Hannah with her baby and her husband and John joined them. From time to time, some straggling acquaintances or old schoolmates would come up to congratulate Rebecca and ask why she had hidden herself in a corner. Then some member of the class would call to her excitedly, reminding her not to be late at the picnic lunch, or begging her to be early at the class party in the evening.

All this had an air of unreality to Rebecca. In the midst of the happy excitement of the past two days, when honors had been falling thick upon her, and behind the delicious exaltation of the morning, had been the feeling that her joy was transient, and that the burden, the struggle, the anxiety, would soon loom again on the horizon. She longed to steal away into the woods with dear old John, grown so manly and handsome, and get some comfort from him.

Meantime Adam Ladd and Mr. Cobb had been having an animated conversation. "I s'pose up to Boston girls like that one are as thick as blackberries?" Uncle Jerry inquired, jerking his head questioningly in Rebecca's direction.

"They may be," smiled Adam, taking in the old man's jovial mood. "Only I don't happen to know one," he said decidedly.

"My eyesight bein' so poor's the reason she looked to be the handsomest girl on the platform, I s'pose?"

"There's no failure in my eyes," responded Adam, "but that was how she seemed to me!"

"What did you think of her voice? Anything extry about it?"

"Made the others sound poor and thin, I thought."

"Well, I'm glad to hear your opinion, you bein' a traveled man, for mother says I'm foolish 'bout Becky an' have been ever since the first. Mother scolds me for spoilin' her, but I notice Mother ain't fur behind when it comes to spoilin'. Land! It made me sick, thinkin' o' them parents travelin' miles to see their younguns graduate, and then when they got here havin' to compare 'em with Becky. Good-by, Mr. Ladd. Drop in some day when you come to Riverboro."

"I will," said Adam, shaking the old man's hand cordially. "Perhaps I'll see you tomorrow if I drive Rebecca home, as I shall offer to do. Do you think Miss Sawyer's condition is serious?"

"Well, the doctor don't seem to know. But anyhow she's paralyzed, and she'll never walk far again, poor soul! She ain't lost her speech; that'll be a comfort to her."

Adam left the church, and in crossing the village green, he came upon Miss Maxwell welcoming old friends and new to Wareham's little campus. Knowing that she was deeply interested in all Rebecca's plans, he told her as he drew her aside that the girl would have to leave Wareham for Riverboro the next day.

"That is almost more than I can bear!" exclaimed Miss Maxwell, sitting down on a bench by the old cannon and stabbing the grass with her folded parasol. "It seems to me that Rebecca never has any rest from her troubles. I had so many plans for her this next month to fit her for her new job. And now she will settle down to housework again and to the nursing of that poor, sick, cross old aunt."

"If it had not been for the 'cross old aunt,' Rebecca would still have been at Sunnybrook. And from the standpoint of educational advantages, or advantages of any sort, she might as well have been in the backwoods," Adam reminded her.

"That is true. I was upset when I spoke, for I thought an easier and happier day was dawning for my prodigy and pearl."

"Our prodigy and pearl," corrected Adam.

"Oh, yes!" she laughed. "I always forget that it pleases you to pretend you discovered Rebecca."

"I believe, though, that happier days are dawning for her," continued Adam. "It must be a secret for the present, but Mrs. Randall's farm will be bought for the new railroad. We must have the right-of-way through the land, and the station will be built on her property. She will receive $15,000, which, though not a fortune, will yield her income enough to live on, if she will allow me to invest it for her. There is a small mortgage on the land. With that paid and Rebecca self-supporting, her mother ought to push for the education of her oldest boy, John, who is a fine, ambitious fellow. He should be relieved from farm work and settled at his studies."

"We might form ourselves into a Randall Protective Agency, Ltd.," mused Miss Maxwell. "I confess I want Rebecca to have a career."

"I don't," said Adam promptly.

"Of course, you don't. Men have no interest in the careers of women! But I know Rebecca better than you."

"You understand her mind better, but not necessarily her heart. You are considering her for the moment as a prodigy, I am thinking of her more as a pearl."

"Well," sighed Miss Maxwell whimsically, "prodigy or pearl, the Randall Protective Agency may pull Rebecca in opposite directions, but, nevertheless, she will follow the Lord in whatever direction He leads, I am sure."

"That will content me," said Adam with grave sincerity.

"Particularly if the Lord points her your way." Miss Maxwell looked up and smiled provokingly.

~ ~ ~

Rebecca did not see her Aunt Miranda until she had been at the brick house for several days. Miranda steadily refused to have anyone but Jane in the room until her twisted face had regained its natural look. But her door was always ajar, and Jane sometimes fancied Miranda liked to hear Rebecca's quick, light step. Miranda's mind was perfectly clear now, and except that she could not move, she was most of the time quite free from pain and alert in every nerve to all that was going on within or without the house. "Are the windfall Duchess apples being picked up for sauce? Are the potatoes thick in the hills? Is the corn tasseling out? Are you keepin' the flypaper hangin' everywheres? Are there any ants in the pantry? Is the kindlin' wood in the shed holdin' out? Has the bank sent the coupons on our investments?" Questions such as these continually flowed from old Miranda's troubled lips.

Poor Miranda Sawyer! Hovering on the verge of eternity, her body, because of her stroke, no longer under the control of her iron will. No divine visions of heaven and

Jesus floated across her tired brain, nothing but her petty cares and sordid anxieties.

The soul can often but with difficulty talk with God, be He ever so near. Poor Miss Miranda—held fast within the prison walls of her own nature, blind in the presence of the revelation of God in the Scriptures and from the pulpit because she had never used the spiritual eye, deaf to the voice of the Holy Spirit because, though religious, she had not used the spiritual ear.

There came a morning when she asked for Rebecca. The door was opened into the dim sickroom, and Rebecca stood there with the sunlight behind her, her hands full of sweet pea blossoms. Miranda's pale, sharp face, framed in its nightcap of flannel, looked haggard on the pillow, and her body was pitifully still under the counterpane.

"Come in," she said. "I ain't dead yet. Don't mess up the bed with them flowers, will ye."

"Oh, no! They're going in a glass pitcher," said Rebecca, turning to the washstand as she tried to control her voice and stop the tears that sprang to her eyes.

"Let me look at ye—come closer. What dress are ye wearin'?" cackled the old aunt in her weak voice.

"My blue calico."

"Is your cashmere holdin' its color?"

"Yes, Aunt Miranda."

"Do ye keep it in a dark closet hung wrong side out, as I told ye?"

"Always."

"Has your mother made her jelly?"

"She hasn't said."

"She always had a knack for writin' letters with nothin' in 'em. What's Mark broken since I've been sick?"

"Nothing at all, Aunt Miranda."

"Why, what's the matter with him? Gettin' lazy, ain't he? How's John turnin' out?"

"He's going to be the best of us all!"

"I hope you don't slight things in the kitchen because I ain't there. Do you scald the coffeepot and turn it upside down on the windowsill every day?"

"Yes, Aunt Miranda."

"It's always yes with you and yes with Jane," groaned Miranda, trying to move her stiffened body. "But all the time I lie here knowin' there's things done the way I don't like 'em."

There was a long pause, during which Rebecca sat down by the bedside and timidly touched her aunt's hand, her heart swelling with tender pity and love at the gaunt face and closed eyes.

"I was dreadfully ashamed to have you graduate in cheesecloth, Rebecca, but I couldn't help it nohow. You'll hear the reason sometime, and you'll know I tried to make it up to ye. I'm afraid you was a laughingstock!"

"No," Rebecca answered. "Ever so many people said my dress and Em's were the very prettiest. They looked like soft lace. You're not to be anxious about anything. Here I am all grown up and graduated — number three in a class of twenty-two, Aunt Miranda — and two positions have been offered me already. Look at me, big and strong and young, all ready to go into the world and show what you and Aunt Jane have done for me. If you want me near, I'll take the teaching job at Edgewood High School, so that I can be here weekends to help. And if you get better, then I'll go to Augusta — for that's a hundred dollars a semester more pay, with music lessons and other responsibilities besides."

"You listen to me," said Miranda quaveringly. "Take the best job regardless of my sickness. I'd like to live long enough to know you'd paid off that mortgage, but I guess I shan't."

Here she ceased abruptly, having talked more than she had for weeks. Rebecca stole out of the room to cry by herself and wonder if old age must be so grim, so hard, so unsweetened as it slipped into the valley of the shadow of death.

The days passed, and Miranda grew stronger and stronger. Her will seemed unassailable, and before long she could be moved into a cane-seated wheelchair by the window. Her dominant thought was to improve enough that the village doctor need not call more than once a week, instead of daily, thereby diminishing the bill that was mounting to such a terrifying sum that it haunted her thoughts by day and her dreams by night.

Little by little hope stole back into Rebecca's young heart. Aunt Jane began to starch her handkerchiefs and collars and purple muslin dress so that Rebecca might be ready to go to Brunswick at any moment when the doctor pronounced Miranda well on the road to recovery. Everything beautiful was to happen in Brunswick with Miss Maxwell if she could be there by August — everything that heart could wish or imagination conceive, for she was to be Miss Emily's very own guest at Bowdoin College and sit at the table with professors and perhaps even meet the famous Harriet Beecher Stowe, whose play she had seen acted so many years before!

At length the day dawned when the few clean, simple dresses were packed into the old leather trunk, with her cheesecloth graduation dress, her class pin, Aunt Jane's lace cape, and the one new hat, which Rebecca tried on every night before going to bed. It was of white chip with a wreath of starched white roses and green leaves, and it cost between two and three dollars, a handsome sum to

Rebecca in those days. The effect of its glories when worn with her nightdress was dazzling enough, but if ever she wore it with the cheesecloth gown, Rebecca felt that even college professors might regard it with respect. It is probable, indeed, that any professorial gaze lucky enough to meet a pair of dark eyes shining under that white-rose garland would never have stopped at respect!

Then all was ready for the trip to Bowdoin College. Abijah Flagg, who was at home from Bowdoin for a week of vacation during the summer, had dropped by to thrill Rebecca with stories of college life. Abijah was about to carry Rebecca's trunk onto the doorstep for Uncle Jerry to take to the train station in Maplewood when there came a telegram from Hannah: "Come at once. Mother has had a bad accident."

In less than an hour, Rebecca had started on her way to Sunnybrook, her heart palpitating with fear as to what might be awaiting her at her journey's end. Death, at all events, was not there to meet her, as it had been on a previous journey to Sunnybrook, but something that looked at first only too much like it. Her mother had been standing on the haymow overseeing some changes her sons were making in the barn. She had slipped, they thought. Her right knee was fractured and her back was strained and hurt when she had fallen to the hard plank floor some fifteen feet below. But she was conscious and in no immediate danger, so Rebecca wrote, when she had a moment to send Aunt Jane the particulars.

"I don' know how 'tis," grumbled Miranda, who was not able to sit up the day Rebecca's letter came from Sunnybrook, "but from a child I never could lay abed without Aurelia's gettin' sick, too. I don't know's she could help fallin', though a haymow ain't any place for a woman, especially one near as old as me. But if it hadn't been that, 'twould 'a' been somethin' else. Aurelia was born unfortunate. Now she'll probably be a cripple the rest of her days, and Rebecca'll have to nurse her instead of earning a good income somewheres else."

"Her first duty is to her mother," said Aunt Jane. "I hope she'll always remember that."

"Nobody remembers anything they'd ought to — at seventeen," responded Miranda. "Now that I'm strong again, there's things I want to consider with you, Jane, things that are on my mind night and day. We've talked 'em over before. Now we'll settle them. When I'm laid away in my grave, do you want to take Aurelia and the children down here to the brick house? There's an awful passel of 'em! But I won't have Mark in the brick house. Hannah and her husband can take him. I won't have a big Randall boy stomping out the carpets and ruinin' the furniture, though I know when I'm dead I can't hinder ye, if you do make up your mind to do anything."

"I shouldn't like to go against your feelings, especially in laying out your money, Miranda," said Jane.

"Don't tell Rebecca I've willed her the brick house until I'm gone. I want to take my time about dying and not be hurried off by them that's going to profit by it. Nor I don't want to be thanked, neither. I suppose she'll use the front stairs as common as the back, and like as not she'll have water piped into the kitchen from the well and one of them fancy new porcelain bathtubs put in. But maybe when I've been dead a few years, I shan't mind.

"Rebecca sets such store by you, she'll want you to have your home here as long as you live," Miranda went on. "But anyway, I've written it down that way, though Lawyer Burns' wills don't hold up in court more'n half the time. He's cheaper, but I guess it comes out just the same in the end. I wasn't going to have the first man Rebecca picks up for a husband turnin' you outdoors."

There was a long pause during which Jane knit silently, wiping the tears from her eyes from time to time as she looked at the pitiful figure lying weakly on the pillows. Then Miranda said slowly and feebly, "Now if you'll draw the curtain, I'll try to sleep."

23

MOTHER AND DAUGHTER

Two months had gone by for Rebecca — two months of steady, exhausting work — of cooking, washing, and ironing. Two months of mending and caring for the three children, although small Jenny was fast becoming a notable little housewife — quick, ready, and capable. Many a weary night Rebecca had watched by her mother, Aurelia. She had soothed and bandaged and rubbed her, had read to her and nursed her, even fed and bathed her.

The ceaseless care was growing less now, and the Randall family breathed more freely, for the mother's sigh of pain no longer came from the stifling bedroom where, during a hot and humid August, Aurelia had lain, suffering with every breath she drew. There would be no question of walking for many a month to come, but on days when the blinds could be opened and the bed drawn near the window, blessings seemed to multiply. When Mother, with pillows behind her, could at least sit and watch the work going on, she could smile at the past agony.

No girl of seventeen can pass through such an ordeal and come out unchanged. No girl of Rebecca's temperament could go through it without some inward unrest and rebellion. She was doing tasks in which she could not be fully happy. These were heavy and trying tasks which perhaps she could never do with complete success or satisfaction, and like a promise of nectar to thirsty lips was the vision of joys she had had to put aside for the performance of dull daily duty. How brief, how fleeting had been those splendid visions when the universe seemed open for her young strength to battle and triumph in! How soon they had faded into the light of common day.

At first, sympathy and grief were so keen that Rebecca thought of nothing but her mother's pain. No consciousness of self interposed between her and her filial service. Then, as the weeks passed, little blighted hopes began to stir and ache in her breast. Defeated ambitions raised their heads as if to sting her; unattainable delights teased her by their very nearness. It is easy for the moment to tread the narrow way, looking neither to the right nor to the left, encouraged by the sense of right doing. But when that first joy of self-denial, the joy that is like fire in the blood, dies away, the path becomes dreary, and the footsteps falter.

Such a time came to Rebecca, and her bright spirit flagged when she received a letter saying that her position in Augusta had been filled by someone else. There was a mutinous leap of her heart then, a beating of the wings against the door of its cage which the Lord had shut for a season, a longing for the freedom of the big world outside. It was the stirring of the powers within her, though she called it by no such grand name. She felt as if the wind of destiny were blowing her flame hither and thither, burning, consuming her from within, but kindling no glorious fires, lighting no grand paths. Though once she'd felt ready to set the world ablaze with the glory of her youth, her little fire could for the moment warm only the lives of the humble family at Sunnybrook.

One stormy night in Rebecca's attic room, the clouds blew from her soul and the sun shone again. She had been reading in the ninetieth Psalm, and in verses twelve through fifteen, she had found these promises:

> Teach us to number our days, that we may apply our hearts unto wisdom. . . . O satisfy us early with thy mercy, that we may rejoice and be glad all our days. Make us glad according to the days wherein thou hast afflicted us.

Rebecca's days were too few to waste on selfish pursuits, she knew. The hours, the days, and the months she had spent with love in her heart tending her mother and Aunt Miranda the Lord would return to her, and in their return fill her with joy and gladness, she could be sure. A rainbow stretched across Rebecca's sky, while hope beckoned her on, saying, "Grow old along with me, The best is yet to be."

Threads of joy ran in and out of the gray, tangled web of Rebecca's daily living. There was the attempt at odd moments to make the bare little house less bare by bringing in the out-of-doors with cut flowers and ferns to cheer her bedridden mother. Then there was the personal satisfaction of being mistress of the Randall household; of planning, governing, deciding; of bringing order out of chaos; of implanting gaiety in the place of dreary resignation.

Another element of comfort was the children's love, for they turned to her as flowers to the sun, drawing confidently on her fund of stories, serene in the conviction that there was no limit to Rebecca's power of make-believe. The children, too, gained confidence and faith through her faith, as she dropped a word here, a verse of Scripture there, to point them to the Lord who had never let her down.

In this and in yet greater things, little as she realized it, the law of compensation was working in Rebecca's behalf, for in those anxious days, mother and daughter found and knew each other as never before. A new sense was born in Rebecca as she hung over her mother's bed of pain and unrest—a sense that comes only from ministering, a sense that grows only when the strong bend toward the weak. As for Aurelia, words could never have expressed her happiness when the real revelation of motherhood was granted her. In all the earlier years when her babies were young, cares and anxieties darkened the fireside with their brooding wings.

Then Rebecca had gone away, and in the long months of silence, Rebecca's mind and soul had grown beyond her mother's narrow experience, so that now, when Aurelia had time and strength to study her child, she seemed to her like some enchanting changeling. Aurelia and Hannah had plodded along in the dull round and the common task. But now, on a certain stage of life's journey, who would appear but this bewildering being, who gave wings to thoughts that had only crept before, who brought color and grace and harmony into the dull brown texture of Aurelia's existence.

You might harness Rebecca to the heaviest plow, but while she had Christ on her side, she would always remember the green earth under her feet and the blue sky over her head. Her physical eye saw the cake she was stirring and the loaf she was kneading. Her physical ear heard the kitchen fire crackling and the teakettle singing, but in faith her fancy mounted on eagle's wings, rested itself, renewed its strength, as she waited on the Lord each day.

The bare little farmhouse was a fixed fact, but Rebecca had many a stately mansion into which she now and then withdrew. These were palaces peopled with stirring and gallant figures belonging to the world of romance and endeavor far beyond the bounds of dear Sunnybrook or the brick house at Riverboro; or, as her heart and mind would carry her, even far beyond the ivy-clad walls of Wareham Academy.

A palace of heavenly counsel, too, Rebecca found in the Word of God. He who is the Way she met there, breathing heavenly counsel as His Spirit guided her into heavenly truth for earthly living. Every time Rebecca retired to meditate and pray she came forth radiant and refreshed, as one who has seen the evening star or heard sweet music or smelled the rose of joy.

Yes, Rebecca had the confidence given her by her education at Wareham Academy, but she had much more. She had the faith in Christ she had learned from the lips of Uncle Jerry, unlearned but wise in spirit. This was a faith which had been nurtured as a small girl by her mother's musings on the Bible and the memorized verses of her Sunday school days, when Mother had been able to take her flock to church in Temperance on the Sabbath.

It was a faith Rebecca had shared with the quiet Aunt Jane, who though she seldom spoke of it, patiently yielded up the fruits of the Spirit. Though to be sure, sometimes these fruits seemed likely to have withered on the vine under Miranda's carping contentions.

Dear old Aunt Miranda! One evening Rebecca mused in the stillness of her room under the eaves, long after she had tucked her two younger sisters into bed and had looked in on her injured mother for the last time that night. Miranda had done her much good, in spite of her self-righteousness, Rebecca knew. How she longed for her to understand God's grace and love. Though Rebecca knew that Miranda had heard the gospel many times in church, she sometimes doubted if she'd ever really received it. Rebecca's heart ached when she contemplated that Aunt Miranda might not live until she returned to the brick house.

Aurelia could have understood the feelings of a narrow-minded and conventional hen who has brought a strange, intrepid duckling into the world. But her situation was still more wonderful, for she could only compare her sensations to those of some quiet, brown wood duck who has brooded an ordinary egg and hatched a bird of paradise. Such an idea had crossed her mind more than once during past weeks, and it flashed to and fro one mellow October morning when Rebecca came into the room with her arms full of goldenrod and flaming autumn leaves.

"Just a hint of the fall styles, Mother," she said, slipping the stem of a gorgeous red and yellow maple sapling between the mattress and the foot of the bed. "This was leaning over the pool by the brook, and I was afraid it would become vain if I left it there too long looking at its beautiful reflection, so I took it away from danger. Isn't it wonderful? How I wish I could carry one to poor Aunt Miranda today! There's never a flower in the brick house when I'm away."

It was a marvelous morning. The sun had climbed into a world that held in remembrance only a succession of golden days and starlit autumn nights. The air was fragrant with ripening fruit, and there was a mad little bird on a tree outside the door nearly bursting his throat with the joy of living. He had forgotten that summer was over, that winter must ever come. And who could think of cold winds, bare boughs, or frozen streams on such a day? A painted butterfly came in at the open window and settled on the tuft of brilliant leaves. Aurelia heard the bird and looked from the beauty of the glowing bush to her tall, splendid daughter, standing like young Spring with golden Autumn in her arms.

Then suddenly she covered her eyes and cried, "I can't bear it! Here I lie as if chained to this bed, interfering with everything you want to do. It's all wasted! All my saving and doing without—all your hard study, all Miranda's outlay. Everything that we thought was going to be the making of you is for nothing."

"Mother, Mother, don't talk so, don't even think so!" exclaimed Rebecca, sitting down impetuously on the floor by the bed and dropping the goldenrod by her side. "Why, Mother, I'm only a little past seventeen! This person in a purple calico apron with flour on her nose is only the beginnings of me! Do you remember the young tree that John transplanted? We had a dry summer and a cold winter, and it didn't grow a bit, nor show anything of all we did for it. Then there was a good year, and it made up for lost time. This is just my rooting season, Mother. Don't go and believe my day is over, because it hasn't begun! The old maple by the well that's in its hundredth year had new leaves this summer, so there must be hope for me at seventeen. God is still in charge—you used to tell me that's what Grandfather Sawyer would say!"

"You can put a brave face on it," sobbed Aurelia, "but you can't deceive me. You've lost your chance at a good job. You'll never see your friends here, and you're becoming nothing but a drudge!"

"I may look like a drudge," said Rebecca mysteriously, with laughing eyes, "but I really am a princess. You mustn't tell, but this is only a disguise."

Aurelia smiled in spite of herself, and though perhaps not wholly deceived, she was comforted.

"I only hope you won't have to wait too long to wear your royal clothes, Rebecca," she said, "and that I shall have a sight of them before I die. But life looks very hard and rough to me, what with your Aunt Miranda a cripple at the brick house, me another invalid here at the farm, and you tied hand and foot, first with the responsibility of one and then with the other, to say nothing of Jenny and Fanny and Mark! You've got something of your father's happy disposition, or it would weigh on you as it does on me."

"Why, Mother!" cried Rebecca, clasping her knees with her hands. "It's enough just to be here in the world on a day like this—to have the chance of seeing, feeling, doing, becoming! When you were seventeen, Mother, wasn't it good just to be alive? You haven't forgotten, have you?"

"No," said Aurelia, "but I wasn't so much alive as you are, never in this world."

"I often think," Rebecca continued, walking to the window and looking out at the trees. "I often think how dreadful it would be if I were not here at all. If Hannah had come, and then, instead of me, John—John and Jenny and Fanny and the others, but no Rebecca, never any Rebecca! To be alive and to know Jesus is directing my life makes up for everything. There ought to be fears in my heart, but there aren't. Something—Someone—stronger sweeps them out like a wind.

"Oh, see! There is Will driving up the lane in his buggy, Mother, and he ought to have a letter from the brick house."

·

24

GOOD-BY SUNNYBROOK

W ill Melville, Hannah's husband, drove up to the window, and tossing a letter into Rebecca's lap, went off to the barn on an errand.

"Sister's no worse, then," sighed Aurelia gratefully, "or Jane would have telegraphed. See what she says."

Rebecca opened the envelope with yesterday's postmark and read in one flash of an eye the whole brief page:

> Your Aunt Miranda passed away an hour ago. Come at once, if your mother is out of danger. I shall not have the funeral till you are here. She died very suddenly and without any pain. Oh, Rebecca! I long for you so!
>
> Aunt Jane

The force of habit was too strong. Even in the hour of death, Jane had remembered that a telegram was a dollar and that Aurelia would have to pay another precious dollar for its delivery, while letters went overnight anywhere in the state for three cents.

Rebecca burst into a passion of tears as she cried, "Poor, poor Aunt Miranda! She is gone without taking a

bit of comfort in life, and I couldn't say good-by to her!
Poor lonely Aunt Jane! What can I do, Mother? I feel torn
in two, between you and the brick house."

"You must go this very instant," said Aurelia, starting
from her pillows. "If I were to die while you were away, I
would say the very same thing. Your aunts have done everything in the world for you — more than I've ever been
able to do — and it is your turn to pay back some of their
kindness and show your gratitude. The doctor says I've
turned the corner, and I feel I have. Jenny can make out
somehow, if Hannah'll come over once a day."

"But Mother, I *can't* go! Who'll turn you in bed?" exclaimed Rebecca, walking the floor and wringing her
hands in anguish.

"It doesn't make any difference if I don't get turned,"
replied Aurelia stoically. "If a woman of my age and the
mother of a family hasn't got sense enough not to slip off
haymows, she ought to suffer. Go put on your black dress
and pack your bag. I'd give a good deal if I was able to go
to my sister's funeral and prove that I've forgotten and
forgiven all she said when I was married. Her acts were
softer'n her words, Miranda's were, and she's made up to
you for all she ever did to hurt me and your father!

"And, oh, Rebecca," she continued with quavering
voice, "I remember so well when we were little girls together, and she took such pride in curling my hair. And
another time, when we were in our teens, she lent me her
best blue muslin dress. Your father had asked me to lead
the grand march with him at the Christmas dance at the
Riverside Grange. To think, I found out afterward she
thought he'd intended to ask her, though she didn't ap-
prove of dancing nor did she particularly like him. But
Miranda was awfully hurt all the same."

Here Aurelia broke down and wept bitterly. The recollection of the past had softened her heart and brought the comforting tears even more effectively than the news of her sister's death.

There was only an hour for preparation. Brother-in-law Will would drive Rebecca to Temperance to catch the next train to Maplewood, and he would send Jenny home from school. He volunteered also to find a neighbor woman to sleep at the farm in case Mrs. Randall should be worse in the night.

Rebecca flew over the hill to get a last pail of water. As she lifted the bucket from the crystal depths and looked out over the glowing beauty of the autumn landscape, she saw a company of railroad surveyors with their instruments making calculations and laying lines that apparently crossed Sunnybrook at her favorite spot where Mirror Pool lay clear and placid, the golden leaves on its surface no yellower than its sparkling sands.

She caught her breath. *The time has come!* she thought. *I am saying good-by to Sunnybrook, and the golden gates that almost swung together that last day in Wareham will close forever now. Good-by dear brook and hills and meadows. You are going to see a new life, too, so we must be hopeful and say to one another, "Grow old along with me, The best is yet to be."*

Will Melville had seen the surveyors, too, and he had heard in the Temperance Post Office that morning a rumor that Mrs. Randall would be made a handsome offer by the railway company for her farm. He was in good spirits at his own improved prospects, for his farm was so placed that its value could only be increased by the new railroad. A siding was planned at his crossroad, it was told, where he and other farmers could ship milk to Portland each day on the morning train from Lewiston, as well as hay for

Boston's livery stables and vegetables for cities throughout
New England.

Will was also relieved at the prospect that his wife's
family would no longer be in dire poverty, directly at his
doorstep, so to speak. Will imagined that John Randall
could now be hurried forward and moved into the position
of head of the family several years sooner than had been
anticipated; perhaps, when his mother was well and his
sisters able to care for themselves, he might even consider
college. In fact, prospects seemed so good to Hannah's
husband that he was obliged to exercise great self-control,
or he would have whistled merrily while he was driving
Rebecca to the station. Will could not understand her sad
face or the tears that rolled silently down her cheeks from
time to time. Hannah had always represented her Aunt Miranda as a cruel, stingy old hag who would be no loss to
the world whenever she should elect to leave it.

"Cheer up, Becky," he said, as he left her at the station. "You'll find your mother sitting up when you come
back, and the next thing you know the whole family'll be
moving to some nice little house wherever your work is.
Things will never be so bad again as they have been this
last year. That's what Hannah and I think." And he drove
away to tell his wife the news.

Adam Ladd was in the station in Temperance and
came up to Rebecca instantly as she entered the door looking very unlike her bright self. "The Princess is sad this
morning," he said, taking her hand. "Aladdin must rub the
magic lamp. Then the slave will appear, and these tears
will be dried in a trice."

He spoke lightly, for he thought her trouble was something connected with affairs at Sunnybrook and he secretly
hoped that he could soon bring the smiles back by telling
her that the farm was sold and that her mother was to re-

ceive a handsome price in return. He meant to remind her, too, that though she must leave the home of her youth, it was too remote a place to be a proper dwelling either for herself or for her lonely mother and the three younger children. He could hear her say as plainly as if it were yesterday, "I don't think one ever forgets the spot where one lived as a child." He remembered well the quaint little figure sitting on the piazza at North Riverboro, and in his mind's eye, he watched her disappear into the lilac bushes when he gave her the memorable order for 300 cakes of Rose Red and Snow White Soap.

A word or two soon told him that her grief was of another sort, and her mood was so absent, so sensitive and tearful, that he could only assure her of his sympathy and ask her permission to visit her soon at the brick house to see with his own eyes how she was faring.

Adam thought, when he had put her on the train and taken his leave, that Rebecca was, in her sad dignity and gravity, more beautiful than he had ever seen her — all-beautiful and all-womanly. But in that moment's speech with her, he had looked into her eyes, and they were still those of a child. There was little knowledge of the world in their shining depths, no mature passion, nor comprehension of it.

He turned from the country railway station to walk in the woods by the wayside until his own train should be leaving. From time to time, he threw himself under a tree to think and dream and look at the glory of the foliage. He had brought a new copy of *Arabian Nights* for Rebecca, wishing to replace the well-worn one that had been the delight of her girlhood. But meeting her at such an inauspicious time, he had absently carried it away with him. He turned the pages idly until he came to the story of "Aladdin and the Wonderful Lamp." And presently, in spite of his nearly thirty years, the old tale held him spellbound as it did in the days when he first read it as a boy.

But there were certain paragraphs that especially caught his eye and arrested his attention—paragraphs that he read and reread, finding in them he knew not what secret delight and significance. These were the quaintly turned phrases describing the effect of the wonderful riches on the once-poor Aladdin, and those describing the beauty and charm of the sultan's daughter, Princess Badroulboudour:

Not only those who knew Aladdin when he played in the streets like a vagabond did not know him again; those who had seen him but a little while before hardly knew him, so much were his features altered. Such were the effects of the lamp, as to procure by degrees to those who possessed it, perfections agreeable to the rank which the right use of it advanced them to.

The Princess was the most beautiful brunette in the world; her eyes were large, lively and sparkling; her looks sweet and modest; her nose was of a perfect proportion and without a fault; her mouth small, her lips of a vermilion red and charmingly agreeable symmetry. In a word, all the features of her face were perfectly regular. It is not therefore surprising that Aladdin, who had never seen, and was a stranger to, so many charms, was dazzled. With all these perfections the Princess had so delicate a shape, so majestic an air, that the sight of her was sufficient to inspire respect.

"Adorable Princess," said Aladdin to her, accosting her and saluting her respectfully, "if I have the misfortune to have displeased you by my boldness in aspiring to the possession of so lovely a creature, I must tell you that you ought to blame your bright eyes and charms, not me."

"Prince," answered the princess, "it is enough for me to have been with you, to tell you that I obey without reluctance."

25

AUNT MIRANDA REPENTS

When Rebecca alighted from the train at Maplewood and hurried to the post office where the stage was waiting, she was filled with joy to see Uncle Jerry Cobb holding the horses' heads.

"The regular driver's sick," he explained, "and when they sent for me, thinks I to myself, my driving days are over, but Becky won't let the grass grow under her feet when she gets her Aunt Jane's letter, and like as not I'll catch her today. If she gets delayed, tomorrow for certain. So here I be just as I was more'n six years ago. Will you be a real lady passenger, or will ye sit up front with me?"

Emotions of various sorts were all struggling together in the old man's face, and the two or three bystanders were astounded when they saw the handsome, stately girl fling herself on Mr. Cobb's dusty shoulder crying like a child.

"Oh, Uncle Jerry!" she sobbed, "dear Uncle Jerry! It's all so long ago, and so much has happened, and we've grown so old, and so much is going to happen that I'm fairly frightened."

"There, there," the old man whispered comfortingly, "we'll be all alone on the stagecoach, and we'll talk things over as we go along the road, an' mebbe they won't look so bad."

Every mile of the way was as familiar to Rebecca as to Uncle Jerry—every well sweep, watering trough, and grindstone; grey-shingled barn and weather vane; duck pond, plank bridge, and sandy brook. All the time she was looking backward to the day, seemingly so long ago, when she sat on the box seat for the first time, her legs dangling in the air, too short to reach the footboard. She could still smell the big bouquet of lilacs, still see the pink-flounced parasol and feel the stiffness of the starched buff calico dress, still remember how it slid on the slick leather seats of the coach. The drive was taken almost in silence, but it was a sweet, comforting silence both to Uncle Jerry and the young woman.

Then came the sight of Squire Bean threshing dry yelloweye beans with a flail in the open door of his barn as they approached Riverboro, and she smiled as she remembered that this would have been Abijah's task had he not begun his fall semester at Bowdoin. Then the Perkins's attic windows came in sight, with a white cloth fluttering from them. Rebecca could sense Emma Jane's loving thought and welcome in that little waving flag—a word and a message sent to her just at the first moment when Riverboro's chimneys rose into view, something to warm her heart till they could meet again.

The brick house on the edge of the village came next, looking just as of yore, though it seemed to Rebecca that death had cast some mysterious spell over it. There were the rolling meadows and the stately elms beside the road in front and long lines of elms that stood like majestic wine glasses along the stone walls that fringed the fields,

*The brick house on the edge of the village came
next, looking just as of yore.*

like the grand guardians of an estate. The elms were yellow and brown, and the shorter maples amongst them glowed bright with red and orange leaves, making the pines among them stand out, a greener green than in summer. She spied, too, the brilliance of the asters in the garden and Aunt Miranda's hollyhocks rising tall against the parlor windows.

In place of the cheerful pinks and reds of the nodding stalks, with their gay rosettes of bloom, however, was a black crepe scarf holding the blinds together, and another on the sitting room side, and another on the brass knocker of the brown-varnished front door.

"Stop, Uncle Jerry! Don't turn in at the drive. Hand me my satchel, please. Drop me in the road and let me run up the path by myself. Then drive away quickly!"

At the noise and rumble of the approaching stage, the door opened from within. Just as Rebecca closed the gate behind her, Aunt Jane came down the split granite steps, a changed woman, frail and broken and white. Rebecca held out her arms, and the aunt who seemed to have grown old suddenly crept into them feebly. Fresh warmth and strength and life flowed into the older frame from the younger one.

"Rebecca," she said, raising her head, "before you go in to look at her, do you feel any bitterness over anything she has ever said to you?"

Rebecca's eyes blazed reproach as she said chokingly, "Oh, Aunt Jane! Could you believe it of me? I am going in with a heart brimful of gratitude!"

"She was a good woman, Rebecca. She had a quick temper and a sharp tongue, but she wanted to do right, and she did it as near as she could."

"I told her before I left that she'd been the making of me, just as Mother says," sobbed Rebecca.

"She wasn't that," said Jane. "God made you in the first place, and you've done consid'rable yourself to help Him along. But she gave you the wherewithal to work with, and that ain't to be despised, 'specially when anybody gives up her own luxuries and pleasures to do it. Now let me tell you something, Rebecca. Your Aunt Miranda's left all of this to you in her will—the brick house and buildings and furniture, and the land all around the house, as far as you can see."

Rebecca smiled through her tears, then her brow furrowed in worry.

"There's something more you should know, Becky," said Aunt Jane softly. "Your Aunt Miranda's taken something with her beyond the grave more valuable than brick houses and fields or orchards."

"You mean?"

"Yes, Rebecca. Miranda called me to her room the day before she died. 'I've made my peace with God at last,' she said," Jane explained. "'But, Miranda, you've always known the Lord,' I told her. 'No, Jane,' she told me as clearly as if she hadn't had a stroke. 'I've been a self-righteous hypocrite. I've resented it when we had to feed the missionaries in the brick house. I did it to keep up appearances. I've been full of pride—proud that our father was a deacon. But Rebecca Randall showed me Jesus' love in a clear and shining way. When Becky asked me once, "Do you really know why Christ died, Aunty dear?" I couldn't answer her. But I've repented now.' Then do you know what Miranda did?"

Rebecca could only shake her head in silence.

"Miranda asked me to get out her will. It was inside your grandfather's Bible, which she had been reading. 'I left Mark Randall out of my will because my heart was filled with bitterness towards his father for marryin' Aurelia instead o' me,' she says. 'Scratch out the part about Mark not comin' into the house.' I crossed it out, and Miranda says, 'Let me see it.' She took the pen from my hand and signed her name beside the change and had me witness it. 'There, that ought to satisfy the judge,' says Miranda. Then she paused, like she was prayin'. 'Jesus satisfied the Judge for me,' Miranda said finally. That was the last words I ever heard her say."

"I'm so happy." said Rebecca, drying her eyes. "Let me go in alone to see her in her casket," she added.

Jane went back to the kitchen to perform the duties which must be done even in a household in mourning. Though Death can stalk through dwelling after dwelling, leaving despair and desolation behind him, the table must be laid, the dishes washed, the beds made by somebody.

Ten minutes later Rebecca came out of the parlor where Aunt Miranda was laid out. Though Rebecca looked white and spent, she seemed chastened and glorified.

Next day, at Aunt Jane's urging, Rebecca wrote her mother, suggesting she sell Sunnybrook Farm and beseeching her earnestly to sell the livestock and move herself and the children to the brick house at Riverboro, though she knew her mother was still infirm and that it might be weeks before she could travel. "Please try to come by Christmas," she wrote. "I'll be back to help you pack in a couple of weeks. Harvest will be over then, and we should be able to gather a good crowd of farmers for an auction. At least please consider it."

During the next several days, Rebecca's time was taken up with putting Aunt Miranda's room in order, packing her keepsakes in a trunk in the attic, and carefully washing and ironing her best everyday clothes for the ladies of the Tory Hill Church's Dorcas Society to give to the poor. Early the second week after her aunt's passing,

Rebecca rested from her labors on the doorstep of the brick house. She had just spent several excruciating hours salvaging the lace from several old silk dresses so the Dorcas ladies could have the cloth for quilting. She sat quietly in the doorway that afternoon, shaded from the little Riverboro world by the stately overhanging elms which grew along the edge of the lawn.

A wide sense of peace and thankfulness possessed her as she viewed the autumn landscape, listened to the rattle of buggy wheels and the clatter of steel-shod hooves on the old plank bridge, and heard the call of the beautiful Saco River as it dashed over the stones toward the sea. She put up her hand softly and touched first the shining brass knocker and then the red bricks, glowing in the glory of the afternoon October sun.

It was home — her roof, her garden, her green acres, her dear trees. It would be shelter for her little family at Sunnybrook. Her mother would have once more the companionship of her sister, Jane, and the friends of her girlhood. The children would have teachers and playmates.

And she? Her own future was close-folded still — folded and hidden in the mind of God, as in beautiful mists, it seemed to her. She leaned her head against the sun-warmed door, and closing her eyes, whispered, "God bless Aunt Miranda; God bless the brick house that was; God bless the brick house that is to be!"

ABOUT THE AUTHORS

K ate Douglas Wiggin (nee Smith, 1856-1923) was born in Philadelphia. As a child she moved with her widowed mother and sister to Portland, Maine, near her mother's birthplace. Kate's mother soon married a country doctor from Hollis, on the Saco, and it was here that Kate grew into her teens.

Kate's mother and stepfather later moved to California, where, in San Francisco, Kate became a founder of the American school kindergarten movement. Back in New England, she married Samuel Wiggin, a Boston lawyer whom she had known as a child in Hollis, Maine. In later life Kate established a summer home in Hollis, and she was awarded an honorary doctorate by Bowdoin College, Brunswick, Maine.

Kate Wiggin's books include *Rebecca of Sunnybrook Farm* (1903) and *New Chronicles of Rebecca* (1906).

Eric E. Wiggin, fifty-one, is a native of Maine, where his books are set, and he formerly was a Maine country pastor and school teacher. He now lives with his wife, Dorothy, and their youngest child, Bradstreet, as a country gentleman in rural Fruitport, Michigan, near where Dot spent her girlhood.

Wiggin has been a Baptist pastor, secondary and college English instructor, and a part-time farmer, carpenter, bus driver, and Maine coastal fish plant worker. He is the editor of contemporary versions of Harvey's *Grammars*, first published in 1868 as companions to *McGuffey's Eclectic Readers*. Wiggin contributes regularly to various evangelical periodicals. He and Dot are the parents of four children (two of them born in Maine) and two grandchildren.